A Murder, a Mystery, and a Marriage

A MURDER, A MYSTERY,

AND A MARRIAGE

BY MARK TWAIN

Foreword and Afterword by Roy Blount Jr.

Illustrations by Peter de Sève

W. W. NORTON & COMPANY
NEW YORK • LONDON

Printed in the United States of America
First published as a Norton paperback 2003

Manufacturing by Quebecor Printing Book Group, Kingsport
Book design by Dana Sloan
Production manager: Julia Druskin

Library of Congress Cataloging-in-Publication Data

Twain, Mark, 1835–1910.
A murder, a mystery, and a marriage / by Mark Twain ; introduction and afterword by Roy Blount Jr. ; illustrations by Peter de Sève.
p. cm.
ISBN 0-393-04376-2
I. Title.

PS1322 .M75 2001
813'.4—dc21 2001041040

ISBN 0-393-32449-4 pbk.

W. W. Norton & Company, Inc.
500 Fifth Avenue, New York, N.Y. 10110
www.wwnorton.com

W. W. Norton & Company Ltd.
Castle House, 75/76 Wells Street, London W1T 3QT

1 2 3 4 5 6 7 8 9 0

Contents

List of Illustrations

TWAIN FACSIMILE PAGES

WATERCOLORS

Foreword

In 1876, when he was forty and the nation a century old, Mark Twain concocted a project, in conjunction with the *Atlantic Monthly*, that came to nothing until 2001. There's a story in that.

"Very often, of course," Mark Twain writes in "How to Tell a Story," "the rambling and disjointed humorous story finishes with a nub, point, snapper, or whatever you like to call it. Then the listener must be alert, for in many cases the teller will divert attention from that nub by dropping it in a carefully casual and indifferent way, with the pretense that he does not know it is a nub. Artemus Ward used that trick a good deal; then when the belated audience presently caught the joke he would look up with innocent surprise, as if wondering what they had found to laugh at."

Twain far more than Ward was a master of such deadpan trickery. Once at a gala banquet, Twain delivered a toast to Ulysses S. Grant that seemed to be a long drawn-out insult. Then he paused "for a sort of shuddering silence" (as he wrote exultantly to his wife, Livy); and then he delivered the snapper. Grant cracked up. "The audience *saw* that for once in his life he had been knocked out of his iron serenity," Twain wrote Livy. "The house came down with a crash."

Another time Twain came onstage and just stood there, expressionless, as if he weren't even aware that he was the speaker. He realized that he could hold people silent on the edge of their seats for just about as long as he wanted to without uttering a word. "An audience captured in that way," he wrote home, "*belongs* to the speaker, body and soul."

But that's not the only silent verdict an audience can render. A few days before the not-yet-notorious presidential election of 1876, Twain's enduringly clueless older brother, Orion Clemens—who had moved just outside slave-state Missouri and declared himself an abolitionist Republican back in the 1850s, when it was unpopular therabouts—suddenly went over to the other party, and was given a chance to speak at a Democratic rally. "He wrote me jubilantly," Twain wrote later to his friend William Dean Howells, "of what a ten-strike he was going to make with that speech. All right—but think of his innocent and pathetic candor in writing me something like this, a week later: 'I was more diffident than I had expected to be, and this was increased by the silence with which I was received when I came forward, so I seemed unable to get the fire into my speech which I had calculated upon, and presently they began to get up and go out, and in a few minutes they all rose up and went away.' How *could* a man uncover such a sore as that and show it to another? Not a word of *complaint*, you see—only a patient, sad surprise."

Twain, too, could be sadly surprised at a rostrum. In 1877 he mortified Howells and himself by his insufficiently reverential attempt to pull the venerable legs of Henry Wadsworth Longfellow, Oliver Wendell Holmes, and Ralph Waldo Emerson—the honored guests at a banquet sponsored by the *Atlantic*. After Howells rose to assure the gathering that here was a humorist who was never offensive, Twain proceeded to spin a long straight-faced western yarn in which Longfellow, Holmes, and Emerson *seemed* to appear as ruffians . . . then came the pause . . . then the snapper . . . and then . . . none of the honorees laughed. (Emerson was not listening in any case.) The audience sat, said Howells, in "silence, weighing many tons to the square inch, which deepened from moment to moment."

But we're getting ahead of our story. When Twain came up with the project that is just now coming to partial fruition, it was around the Ides of March, 1876. He proposed to Howells, who was then editor of the *Atlantic*, that they round up "a good and godly gang" of authors—including the preeminent Boston Brahmins James Russell Lowell and Holmes, the recently lionized mining-camp local colorist (from Albany, New York) Bret Harte, and the young Henry James—who would each write a story based on one "skeleton" plot devised by Twain. The stories would appear serially in the *Atlantic*, the nation's foremost bastion of literary standards. Throughout the rest of that year, Twain kept urging Howells to get this unlikely project off the ground. Howells sent out feelers. (Though evidently not to anyone so august as Holmes or Lowell. When Howells had taken Twain to meet Lowell two years before, that worthy had not been impressed, except that something about Twain's nose lent fuel to Lowell's belief that all humanity was descended from the Jews.) "The difficulty" about the stories, as Howells put it, was "to get people to write them."

During that very period, history was holding its breath. Two projects of enormously greater importance than Twain's "skeleton novelette" were in abeyance. Rutherford B. Hayes and Samuel Tilden were pitted in a presidential race whose muddled outcome would have to be resolved by deal making in and out of the House of Representatives. And Twain himself got stuck halfway through

The Adventures of Huckleberry Finn—lost interest, said he might burn the manuscript.

Two great, and not unrelated, turning points in American history and culture. The result of the 1876 election would be seen as a betrayal of the verdict of the Civil War. As it turned out, Tilden won the popular vote—thanks in good measure to intimidation of southern blacks, who would have voted Republican—and Hayes won the electoral vote by a 185–184 margin—if you counted results in three states that were contested and weren't ever going to be recounted impartially. An Electoral Commission was formed, which voted for Hayes, strictly along party lines. Tilden's Democrats in the House mounted a filibuster. So Hayes's Republicans agreed to pull out of the South the Federal troops that had been enforcing Reconstruction. The party of Lincoln thus relinquished its commitment to advancing the rights and opportunities of African Americans, who had been emancipated but were still far from being included in common American advantages. That 1876 election has often been cited in regard to our most recent, chad-splitting presidential imbroglio, whose outcome has led to apprehension or anticipation that affirmative action, a fruit of the civil rights movement, will be abandoned as a federal goal. If Reconstruction had worked as planned, we wouldn't have *needed* a civil rights movement a hundred years after the war.

And what if Twain had neglected to finish his masterpiece? That novel—in which a poor, good-natured white boy from a slave state comes to respect and assist a runaway slave, in defiance of all the dictates of antebellum society—would blend standard English and New World vernacular, black and white, into the template of American narrative. All modern American literature, Ernest Hemingway would say in 1935, began with that book.

If we could come up with a skeleton plot for the quintessential American writer's career, wouldn't it call for him to realize the momentousness of 1876? Twain was himself a refugee from a slave state and indeed the Confederate Army. His earliest storytelling influence was a slave named Uncle Daniel, who would weave a ghostly web and then *jump out* at the black and white children gathered around him. Twain's first contribution to the *Atlantic*, published in 1874, was a poignant tale in the form of an ex-slave's monologue, "A True Story." The *Atlantic*, though culturally conservative and independent of party affiliation, had firmly supported the abolitionist Republican position before and during the war. Now both Reconstruction and the Great American Novel were hanging in the balance. And yet, judging from the letters back and forth between Twain and Howells at the time, what was weighing most heavily on Twain's mind was *A Murder, a Mystery, and a Marriage*, the skeletal project that never went beyond the story you are about to read.

He got coy about showing his odd fiction to Howells—whether he ever did, and exactly what became of the manuscript over the next seventy years or so, is unclear. In 1945 two men who had bought the manuscript from an auction house printed up sixteen copies in hopes of establishing copyright, but the Twain estate sued to prevent publication, and a court decided in 1949 that the work could not be published. In 2000, the Buffalo and Erie County Public Library acquired the rights to publish the work. This links the story in another way to the separate halves of *Huckleberry Finn*. In 1885, the year the novel was finally published (he hadn't returned to writing it until 1879 or 1880), the Young Men's Association Library in Buffalo, New York, which later became the Buffalo and Erie County Public Library, asked Twain to donate the manuscript to its collection. Twain, who had lived briefly in Buffalo some fifteen years before, replied that as far as he knew the first half had been destroyed by the printer, but he sent the second half on. One hundred and five years later, the first half was discovered, in an attic in of all places Hollywood, California. Researchers on the staff of the Mark Twain Papers in the Bancroft Library at the University of California then dug up an 1887 letter in which Twain said he had found the first half after all and was forwarding it to the Young Men's Association Library. The curator there meant to get the first half bound, but he didn't get around to it. When he died, the manuscript was left in a trunk, which his widow conveyed to Hollywood in the 1920s when she moved there to be close to her daughter. So now the two halves of the handwritten *Huckleberry Finn* are together in Buffalo, and they are joined by one of the distractions that kept the writing of them apart.

Over the years *A Murder, a Mystery, and a Marriage* has been ignored almost entirely by the myriad scholars who have scrutinized every other scrap of Twain's writing voluminously. *Mark Twain A to Z*, a reliable and comprehensive book of reference, confuses it with an earlier, unfinished piece.

Now, the story seems more interesting. Does it reflect in any way Twain's deepest concerns? What made him want to share it with such a disparate band of writers? (Particularly, *Henry James*?) Why did Twain give one of its meanest characters, David Gray, the name of a sweet-natured friend of his? What was he *thinking*? And what were Mark Twain's politics, anyway?

An afterword to the story will fill in the history of Twain's project and attempt to answer the questions that it raises, including what mugwumpery meant to Twain and what his mark may have been on another great American novel, whose plot has to do with determining and influencing the leanings of a dangling or disconnected character named, as it happens, Chad.

But here, with illustrations by Peter de Sève, is *A Murder, a Mystery, and a Marriage* by Mark Twain, published for the first time in book form.

—Roy Blount Jr.
Mill River, Massachussetts

A Murder, a Mystery, and a Marriage

A Murder, a Mystery, & a Marriage.

Upon the border of a remote & out-of-the-way village in south-western Missouri lived an old farmer named John Gray. The village was called Deer Lick. It was a straggling, drowsy hamlet of ~~three~~ six or seven hundred inhabitants. These people knew, in a dim way, that out in the great world there were things called railways, steamboats, telegraphs & newspapers, but they had no personal acquaintance with them, ~~& no tr~~ & took no more interest in them than they did in the concerns of

CHAPTER ONE

UPON THE BORDER OF A REMOTE AND OUT-OF-THE-WAY village in south-western Missouri lived an old farmer named John Gray. The village was called Deer Lick. It was a straggling, drowsy hamlet of six or seven hundred inhabitants. These people knew, in a dim way, that out in the great world there were things called railways, steamboats, telegraphs and newspapers, but they had no personal acquaintance with them, and took no more interest in them than they did in the concerns of the moon. Their hearts were in hogs and corn. The books used in the primitive village school were more than a generation old; the aged Presbyterian minister, Rev. John Hurley, still dealt in the fire and brimstone of an obsolete theology; the very cut of the people's garments had not changed within the memory of any man.

John Gray, at fifty-five, was exactly as well off as he was when he had inherited his small farm thirty years before. He was able to grub a living out of his land, by hard work; by no amount of endeavor had he ever been able to do more. He had had ambitions toward wealth, but the hope of acquiring it by the labor of his hands had by slow degrees died within him and he had become at last a blighted, querulous man. He had one chance left, and only one. This was, the possibility of marrying his daughter to a rich man. He observed with content, that an intimacy had sprung up between Mary Gray and young Hugh Gregory; for Hugh, in addition to being good, respectable and diligent, would be left tolerably well off whenever his aged father's days should come to an end. John Gray encouraged the young man, from selfish motives; Mary encouraged him because he was tall, honest, handsome, and simple-hearted, and because she liked curly auburn hair better than any other. Sarah Gray, the mother, encouraged him because Mary liked him. She was willing to do anything that might please Mary, for she lived only in her and for her.

Hugh Gregory was twenty-seven years old, Mary twenty. She was a gentle creature, pure in heart, and beautiful. She was dutiful and obedient, and even her father loved her as much as it was in him to love anything. Presently Hugh began to come daily to see Mary; he and she took long horseback rides when the weather was pleasant, and in the evenings they had cosy confidential chats together in a corner of the parlor while the old people and Mary's youthful brother Tom kept to themselves by the fireplace and took no notice. John Gray's nature was softening fast. He gradually ceased to growl and fret. His hard face took to itself a satisfied look. He even smiled now and then, in an experimental way.

One stormy winter's night Mrs. Gray came beaming to bed an hour later than her husband, and whispered:

"John, everything's safe at last. Hugh has popped the question!"

John Gray said:

"Say it again, Sally, say it again!"

She said it again.

"I want to get up and hurrah, Sally. It's too good for anything! *Now* what'll Dave say! Dave may go to grass with his money—nobody cares."

"Well, old man, nobody does care. And it's well it's so, because if your brother ever might have left us his money he'll never do it now, because he hates Hugh like p'ison—has hated him ever since he tried to cheat Hugh's father out of the Hickory Flat farm and Hugh chipped in and stopped the thing."

"Don't you worry about any money we've lost of Dave's, Sally. Since the day I quarreled with Dave, twelve years ago, he has hated me more and more all the time and I've hated him more and more. Brothers' quarrels don't heal, easy, old wife. He has gone on getting richer and richer and richer, and I've hated him for that.

I'm poor, and he's the richest man in the county—and I hate him for *that.* Much money Dave would be likely to leave to us!"

"Well, you know he used to pet Mary a good deal before you quarreled, and so I thought maybe—"

"Shaw! 'Twas an old bachelor's petting—no money in it for Mary—you can depend on that. And if there might have been, it's all up with it, now, as you say; for he wouldn't give her a cent that Hugh Gregory might ever get hold of."

"Dave's a mean old hunks, anyway you can fix him, pap. I wish there was some other place where Hugh could sleep when he is in the village over night but in the same building with David Gray. Hugh's father has tried to get Dave to move his office out of there, time and time again, but he sticks to his lease. They say he is always at the front door of a morning, ready to insult Hugh when he comes down stairs. Mrs. Sykes told me she heard Dave insult Hugh one morning about six weeks ago, when three or four people were going by. She looked to see Hugh break his head, but he didn't. He kept down his temper, and never said anything but 'Mr. Gray, you might do this thing once too often, one of these days.' Dave sneered at him and said, 'O yes, you've said that before— why don't you *do* something? what do you talk about it so much for?'"

"Well, we'll go to sleep, old woman. I reckon things are going about right with us at last. Here's luck and long life to Hugh and Mary—*our* children— God bless 'em!"

Chapter Two

About eight o'clock the next morning the Rev. John Hurley rode up to John Gray's gate, hitched his horse and ascended the front steps. The family heard him stamping the snow off his boots, and Mr. Gray delivered a facetious glance at Mary and said:

"Seems to me Hugh comes a little earlier and a little earlier every morning, don't he, honey?"

Mary blushed and her eyes sparkled with a proud pleasure, but these things did not keep her from flying to the door to welcome—the wrong man. When the old clergyman was come into the presence of the family, he said:

"Well, friends, I've got some splendid news for ye!"

"Have you, though?" said John Gray. "Out with it, Dominie, and I'll agree to cap it with better news still, which I'll give *you*."

He cast a teasing glance at Mary, who dropped her head. The old minister said:

"Good—my news first and yours afterward. You know, David Gray has been down on the South Fork for a month, now, looking after his property there. Well the other night he staid at my son's house, there, and in the talk it came out that he made his will about a year ago and in it he leaves every cent of his wealth to—whom do you suppose? Why, to our little Mary here—nobody else! And you can depend on it I didn't lose a minute after reading my son's letter. I rushed right here to tell you—for, says I to myself, this will join those estranged brothers together again, and in the mercy of God my old eyes shall see them at peace and loving each other once more. I have brought you back the lost love of your youth, John Gray—now cap it with better news if you can! Come, tell me your tidings!"

All the animation had passed out of John Gray's face. It was hard, troubled, distraught. One might have supposed he had just heard of a crushing calamity. He fumbled with his garments, he avoided the inquiring eyes that were fixed upon him, he tried to stammer out something, and failed. The situation was becoming embarrassing. To relieve it, Mrs. Gray came to the rescue with—

"*Our* great news is that our Mary here—"

"Hold your tongue, woman!" shouted John Gray.

The simple mother shrank away, dumb. Mary was confused and silent. Young Tommy Gray retired the back way, as was his custom when his father showed temper. There was nothing to be said; consequently nobody said anything. There was a most awkward silence for a few moments, and then the old clergyman made his way out of the place with as little ease and as little grace as another man might who had got a kick where he looked for a compliment.

John Gray walked the floor for ten minutes rumpling his hair and growling savagely to himself. Then he turned upon his cowed wife and daughter and said:

"Mind you—when Mister Gregory comes for his answer, tell him it is *no!* Do you hear? Tell him it is No. And if you can't muster pluck enough to tell him I'd rather he wouldn't come here any more, leave it to me. I'll tell him."

"O, father, you don't mean to say—"

"Not a word out of you, Mary! I *do* mean to say it. There, now. Just drop the matter."

With that, he flourished out of the house, leaving Mary and her mother in tears and heart broken. It was a brilliant winter morning; the level prairie that stretched abroad from John Gray's house to the horizon, was a smooth white floor of snow. It was just as the storm of the night before had left it—unmarred by track or break of any kind.

John Gray plowed his way through the snow straight out into

the prairie, never noting what direction he took, nor caring. All he wanted was room to relieve his mind. His thought ran somewhat after this fashion:

"Just my luck! This thing *would* turn up exactly at the wrong time, of course! But it ain't too late, it ain't too late, yet. Dave shall soon know that there ain't anything in the talk about Mary and Gregory—if he has heard it, but I know he hasn't, else he'd have snatched her out of his will in a minute. No, he shall know that nobody of the tribe of Gregory can have Mary—or look at her, even. One good thing, she'll never say yes to him or any other man till she knows I'm willing. I'll send Mr. Gregory a-tramping, in short order! And I'll mighty soon let everybody know it, too. What's Gregory's money to Dave's! Dave could buy all the Gregorys twenty times over, and have money left. Just let it be spread around that Mary is to have Dave's money and she can take her pick and choice in six counties around. Hello, what's this!"

It was a man. A young man, under thirty, by his looks, dressed in a garb of unfamiliar pattern, and lying at full length in the snow; motionless, he was—evidently insensible. His dress had a costly look about it, and he had several jewels and trinkets upon his person. Near him lay a heavy fur coat and a couple of blankets, and at a little distance a valise. About him the snow was somewhat tumbled, but everywhere else it was still smooth. John Gray cast his eye around for the horse or the vehicle that had brought the stranger,

"Here was indeed a wonder."

but nothing of the kind was to be seen. Moreover, there was no track of wheels or horse, or of any man, either, save the tracks he had made himself, in coming from his house. Here was indeed a wonder. How did the stranger get there, more than a quarter of a mile from a road or a house, without breaking the snow, or leaving a track? Had the hurricane blown him thither?

But this was no time to be inquiring into details; something must be done. John Gray put his hand into the stranger's breast; it was still warm. He fell to chafing the chilled temples. He towsled and tumbled his patient, and rubbed snow on his face. Signs of life began to appear. John Gray's eye fell upon a silver flask that lay in the snow by the blankets. He seized it and poured some of its contents between the stranger's lips. The effect was encouraging; the man stirred a trifle, and heaved a sigh. John Gray continued his efforts; he raised the man to a sitting posture, and presently the closed eyes opened and gazed around with a dazed, lack-lustre expression. Next they dwelt a moment upon John Gray's face and something more of life came into them.

"I wish he'd speak," said Gray to himself. "I've a powerful hankering to know who he is and how he got here. Good—he *is* going to speak!"

The lips parted, and after an effort or two, these words came forth:

"*Ou suis-je?*"

The eager expectancy in John Gray's eyes faded out and left his face looking blank enough. He was grievously disappointed.

"What kind of jabber might that be?" said he to himself.

He quickened the stranger's consciousness with another draught from the flask. The handsome foreign eyes peered perplexedly into John Gray's a moment, and then this question followed:

"*Wo bin ich?*"

John Gray stared stupidly, and shook his head.

"It ain't a Christian," thought he; "maybe it ain't a human. I'd think so if it wasn't for its harness; but—"

"*Donde estoy? Dove sono? Gdzie ja jestem?*"

A sorely bothered expression spread its blank expanses over John Gray's face, and the stranger perceived, with plainly apparent distress, that once more he had failed to make himself understood. He struggled to raise himself to his feet; he undermined John Gray's already tottering reason with a succession of graceful but complex signs drawn from the deaf and dumb language; then he began to rail at Gray, in a peculiarly barbarous foreign tongue for idling there and looking stupid when he ought to be bestirring himself and giving all the help he could to an unfortunate stranger. For the first time Gray spoke aloud. Said he:

"By George, he's woke up at last! And he's woke up all over, too. There ain't no doubt about—"

"O, you're English! you're English! Good! Why didn't you say so? Come, bear a hand! help me up! I'm worth twenty dead men, yet! Pound me, rub me, kick me! Give me brandy!"

The amazed farmer obeyed orders vigorously, under the spur of the stranger's commanding tones, and meantime the patient's tongue ran on, sometimes in one language, sometimes in another. Finally he made a step or two, leaning upon Gray, then stopped and said in English:

"My friend, where am I?"

"Where are you? Why you're in my prairie. You're in the edge of Deer Lick. Where did you think you was?"

"Prairie? Deer Lick?" said the stranger, musingly. "I don't know these. What *country* am I in?"

"What *country*? Why, dern it all, you ain't in *any* country. You're in Missouri. And it's the banner State of America, I reckon."

The stranger put his hands impressively upon John Gray's shoulders, held him at arms' length a moment, looked him steadily in the eyes, then nodded his head two or three times, as if satisfied. An hour later he was in bed at John Gray's house, tossing to and fro in a restless sleep, burning up with a fever, and murmuring brokenly, and ceaselessly, in nearly all languages but English. Mary, her mother, and the village doctor, were working over him faithfully.

I'll send Mr. Gregory a-tramping, in short order! And I'll mighty soon let everybody know it, too. What's Gregory's money to Dave's! Dave could buy all the Gregorys twenty time over, & have money left. Just let it be spread around that Mary is to have Dave's money & she can take her pick & choice in six counties around. Hello, what's this!"

It was a man. A young man, under thirty, by his looks, dressed ~~in an outlandish garb~~ in a garb of unfamiliar pattern, & lying at full length in the snow; motionless, he was—evidently in-

Chapter Three

WE SKIP SIX MONTHS, AND GO ON WITH OUR HISTORY. The old clergyman had tried hard to unite the two brothers, but had failed. David Gray had firmly declined to make or receive overtures. He said he had no liking for any member of his brother's family but Mary.

Mary Gray had permitted herself to steal one interview with Hugh Gregory, simply to assure him that whatever her duty to her father might oblige her to do, her love for Hugh would remain perfect, undiminished, while she lived. There was an exchange of pictures and locks of hair, a distressful parting, and there an end. The lovers glimpsed each other at church and other places, now and then, but there was seldom an interchange of glances, and never of speech. Both seemed listless, and tired of life.

Meantime the stranger had risen into great prominence. He had set up as a teacher of languages, music, and a little of everything else that was new and marvelous to that backwoods community. For a while he had remained mysteriously silent about his origin; but gradually he dropped a word or two privately into the ears of the Grays while he was recovering from his illness. After he had become well his visits to the house were frequent and welcome; for he had a high-bred grace of deportment which was the envy and admiration of everybody, and a tongue that could fascinate a graven image. He compelled Mary Gray's regard by his gentleness, his considerate ways, the purity of his sentiments,—his vast knowledge, his adoration of poetry; the old people were charmed by the respect, indeed the reverence, which marked his conduct towards them; he was always astounding the boy Tom with marvelous inventions in the way of scientific toys, so Tom was his devoted ally. By driblets Mr. George Wayne—for so he called himself—made himself known to the old people confidentially, and they confidentially delivered the facts to their particular friends, who straightway conferred them confidentially upon the community at large. One night Mrs. Gray brought some fresh news to bed with her. She said:

"John, I've been having such a talk with Mr. Wayne! What do you think? Now don't you ever tell—not a word to anybody—don't you ever let on to *him,* even—because he said it wouldn't ever do to let it be known."

"Out with it you old fool, out with it! I'll keep mum."

"Well, you know he used to always shet up like a shell whenever we asked him what countryman he was. Times we've thought he was an I-talian, then a Spaniard, and times we thought maybe he was an A-rab. But he ain't. He's a Frenchman. He told me so. And that ain't all, by a grand sight. His family is awful rich and grand."

"No! is that so? I always said it to myself. 'Deed I always said it."

"And that ain't all, either. His father's a lord!"

"No!"

"Yes! And *he's* a lord, too!"

"Great Caesar!"

"True as you're a laying there, he said it. He's a Count! Think of that!"

"By George! But what did he leave home, for?"

"That's what I'm a coming at. His father wanted him to marry a grand girl, for her wealth and high style. He wouldn't; said he'd marry for love or not at all. Then they had words. Then there was some politics mixed up in it. This one is down on the king, or the emperor, or whatever he is, and it got found out, and he had to clear the country. He dassn't go back for two years, he says—till the law's time's up—or they'll fling him into prison and make him pay like smoke besides."

Mr. Gray sat up in bed, pretty thoroughly excited.

"Old woman, I wish I may never stir if I haven't said to myself forty times, 'This pelican's a king or something!' It's so, b'George! I just knowed it; something seemed to tell me so. Thunder, but this is a go!"

"Well, *I* always thought there was something kinder uncommon and gaudy about him, too."

"Old woman"—in a low voice—"don't you know, he's got his eye on our Mary? Say, don't you know that?"

"Well, as you say, I've kinder thought it, sometimes—but then, he's up so high, and so rich—"

"Never you mind about that. Didn't he tell his old father he wouldn't ever marry, only for love? You encourage him, that's all. And I will, you bet."

"But husband, she's just a-wasting away for poor Hugh—and if it only *could* be, I do wish—"

"Hang poor Hugh! That was a good escape. A mighty good escape. You want to do the best you can by your daughter, don't you? Well, I do, too. Think of her being a grandee's wife like that! Don't you know she wouldn't worry long about Hugh Gregory? Why of course. Say—what's his *real* name?"

"Mind, husband, you're never to tell. It's Count Hubert dee Fountingblow. Ain't it a sweet name?"

"Well, I bet it is. Blamed if I don't wish *I* had a handle like that. John Gray! My name ain't fitten for a rat! Look here, Sally, it ain't going to do to ever let go a single word about him being a

Count. Not a word. All the girls in forty miles around would be after him."

There was some more talk. Then by and by the conversation drifted into the Count's relations with Hugh Gregory. It appeared that the two young men had become pretty intimate with each other, and frequently visited each other's rooms. Mrs. Gray said she had heard that the Count had tried several times to patch up a peace between Hugh and old David Gray, but had failed every time. David had become pretty fond of the Count, and liked to have him visit his office and talk, but steadily refused to make up with young Gregory.

By and by Mr. and Mrs. Gray ceased to chat, and began to drop off to sleep. At this point John Gray suddenly roused up and whispered hoarsely in his wife's ear:

"Say, Sally, there's one more thing. From the very day that I found young Mr. Fountingblow out yonder in the snow, we've all pegged at him in one way or another, to tell how he got there without making a track—but he always shet himself up and swapped off onto something else when we got to that. Come—how *did* he get there? Did he say?"

"No. Said he'd ruther tell by and by. Said it might get around, and he had reasons for not wanting it. But he said he'd tell *us* by and by."

"Well, all right, if it can't be helped. I'll sweat it out a spell longer, but I'm just a-busting to know."

CHAPTER FOUR

THERE WAS A LEAKY VESSEL SOMEWHERE. WITHIN A WEEK everybody was talking in whispers about "Count Fontainebleau" and his incredible riches. People were saying, also, that the Count was paying marked attentions to Mary Gray, and that John Gray was strongly and his wife feebly urging Mary to look with favor upon his suit.

In truth Mary was in a good deal of trouble. She was trying hard to mould herself to her parents' wishes, but nightly and in secret she found herself kissing a certain picture and crying over a certain lock of hair.

One day the Count spent an hour with David Gray, in his office, chatting about various matters. He led gradually up toward the subject of matrimony, and was finally about to speak of his hopes with regard to Mary Gray when David was suddenly called out. The Count listlessly amused himself with inspections of such odds and ends of documents as lay around or were exposed in half-open drawers. One paper he read with great interest, then said,—

"It was just as well to make sure; and now I am satisfied. It was a false report."

He took his leave and wended toward John Gray's house. He sought Mary and was told she was in the orchard. He went thither, and wandered among the paths, until, in a remote corner of the place he caught a glimpse of female apparel protruding from behind a tree where was a rustic bench which was large enough to seat two persons and had been very useful at times during the past twelve-month. He approached, and appeared suddenly to Mary. She hastily concealed Hugh Gregory's picture in her bosom, then rose with her handkerchief to her eyes—for she was crying.

"Mary, my honored, my worshiped friend," said the Count, taking her hand in his courtly way, "Your poor heart is breaking, and I am the cause. O, it was a fatal thing that I knew you before I knew that you loved—him. To see you was to love you. None could help that. Afterward, when I found that your father had forbidden that marriage, I felt that my love for you could no longer be a wrong toward you or toward poor Hugh. I insanely hoped that you might come, by and by, to give me a place in your heart. But I fear it can never be. Your tears, your grief, are for Hugh, and heaven knows he

"I must try to give you up, for your sake whom I love better than life!"

is worthy. I must try to give you up. For your sake, whom I love better than life, fortune, repute,—better than my own soul!—I must try to do this impossible thing! Do not speak, I beseech you!—I cannot hear the music of your voice and maintain my resolution. I am a creature of impulse. The spectacle of your distress, this moment witnessed by me, has suddenly wrought within me the power to do this act of self-sacrifice, and as suddenly must I perform it and take myself from the sight of your face and the sound of your voice, or I fail. I go—I make my endeavor—God send me a speedy death!—it is all I ask! O, not a word! not a word, I implore you! Farewell, I yield you up, my precious one! My darling, my darling, farewell, and God keep you!"

With his handkerchief to his face, he was flying toward the house the next instant. Mary Gray, standing like one paralyzed, gazed after him until he had disappeared, then she said, sobbing:

"O, how little I knew him! He is a thousand times nobler by nature than the highest blood and the oldest ancestry could make him. Five minutes ago I almost hated him. Now—why now I could almost—love him! O, I shall respect him, honor him, reverence him, all the days of my life—great, pure, noble heart!"

Chapter Five

During three days the Grays saw nothing of the Count. The father and mother wondered, but said little, for they observed that Mary was in better spirits than usual, wherefore they judged that matters must be improving between her and the Count.

About the fall of evening, on the third day, the Count was standing on a village corner holding a moment's conversation with David Gray when Hugh Gregory passed by; stopped; hesitated; returned and asked the Count if he should be going to his lodgings presently. Before the Count could reply, David Gray said:

"Don't waste your time with me, Count, when there's better and purer and sweeter people to associate with. I'll let you go at once."

"Do you mean that for me, sir?" said Hugh.

Several passers-by stopped to listen.

"Yes, I *do* mean it for you, my peach. *You* didn't stop here to make that remark to the Count. You stopped here because you thought it would aggravate *me.* You know you did. You're always doing it. You think maybe I don't know you. It was the like of *you* that wanted Mary Gray, was it? All for love, too, I reckon—didn't have any idea I was going to leave her my little savings. O, of course not! But I'll show you a thing or two, my lad. If I live forty-eight hours I'll make a new will and leave Mary Gray clear out of it. Don't scowl at me like that, my friend, I won't put up with it."

"It is useless to bandy words with a lunatic," said Hugh, with a forced calmness. "I will take my—"

The irascible old man's cane crashed down upon Hugh's head as he turned upon his heel, making him stagger, and interrupting his remark. The next instant Hugh's fist shot from his shoulder and stretched David Gray at his length upon the ground. In a frenzy of anger Hugh sprang forward to continue the assault, but was seized by several persons and borne from the place, he struggling to free himself, and exclaiming, "Let me at him, let me at him! he has insulted me brutally fifty times and nothing shall stop me from squaring the account!"

"Let me at him! Let me at him!"

Chapter Six

About ten o'clock the next morning the Count entered John Gray's house, and John Gray's heart was glad once more. His lordship looked worn, weary and wretched. He said:

"Absence from this house is misery; there is no happiness but here! My heart hungers—let me see Mary!"

The prayer was promptly answered; Mary came, the others went. The Count said:

"O, I had to come—I could not live where you were not! I tried so hard—for your sake—to give you up, but it was beyond my strength. Look at me—behold in every hair of my head and every feature of my face a witness of the tortures I have endured. I could not sleep, I could not rest. I have come to throw myself upon your mercy—to plead for your compassion, to beg for my life. I cannot live without you. I have tried so hard, so cruelly hard—and failed. Have pity upon me!"

Mary's compassion was stirred to the depths, her tears fell like rain. She tried to say comforting things; he answered with passionate beseechings. So the sorrowful struggle went on, till John Gray burst into the room and exclaimed:

"David is murdered! Hugh Gregory is in jail for it!"

Mary swooned away.

All day the village was in a turmoil. All occupations were suspended. Crowds stood for hours in front of David Gray's office, talking about the murder, and waiting patiently for chance opportunities to enter and stare at the grisly spectacle within. The dead man lay in a sea of blood. The overturned furniture showed that there had been a struggle. On the desk lay a sheet of legal cap upon which David Gray had begun a sentence, but had not lived to finish it—to wit:

"I, David Gray, being of sound mind and—"

Near the corpse had been found a fragment of cloth which exactly fitted a vacant corner of Hugh Gregory's coat-skirt; several very small sprinkles of blood had been found upon Hugh's pantaloons; here lay the opening sentence of a will which was to sweep away the prospective fortune of the girl whom Hugh Gregory was hoping to marry some day; it was whispered that Hugh's father had

David Gray's office, talking about the murder, & waiting patiently for chance opportunities to enter & stare at the grisly spectacle within. The dead man lay in a sea of blood. The overturned furniture showed that there had been a struggle. ~~[illegible]~~ On the desk lay a sheet of legal cap upon which David Gray had begun a sentence, but had not lived to finish it—to-wit:

"I, David Gray, being of sound mind and—"

In ~~[illegible]~~ the murdered man's ~~hands~~ grasp had been found ~~some~~ half a handful of curly auburn hair—plainly ~~Hugh~~ Gregory's, everybody said.

lately been getting into dangerously deep water, financially; the rencontre of the evening before was dilated upon; somebody brought up a remark which Hugh had once made, that David Gray would revile and insult him "once too often, some day."

Plainly Hugh Gregory was the murderer. Everybody admitted that, and grieved over it. Most people believed, however, that he had been moved by no sordid impulse, but by an uncontrollable desire for vengeance for long-continued injuries. Hugh declared his innocence stoutly, in the face of the fatal array of circumstantial evidences which pointed to him as the criminal. The declaration of his innocence had such a seemingly honest ring about it that it made some of the villagers waver in their beliefs for a while, but only a while; for about the middle of the afternoon a bloody knife, well known to belong to Hugh was found secreted in the foot of his feather bed; a trifling little red stain upon the ticking had called attention to the small rip which had been made for the purpose of admitting the knife.

No human being believed in Hugh Gregory's innocence, now, except Mary Gray, and her confidence was diminishing. Hugh sent her a letter imploring her to have faith in his guiltlessness, for that God would surely reveal it in His good time, out of His great grace; but this letter tarried in John Gray's hands and went no further. During several days Mary Gray waited in misery for an answer to a note which she had written to Hugh begging him to give her a word of comfort; but no answer came—to her. Tommy Gray had promised to smuggle Mary's letter into Hugh's hands and had accomplished his mission; but the elder Gray had his eye on the boy; he captured the reply and easily terrified the boy to that degree that he was glad to report to Mary that Hugh had crumpled her letter in his hands and declared that if she really loved him she would be moving heaven and earth for his rescue instead of fooling away precious time in inquiries concerning his guilt or innocence. Several days and nights of anguish followed, with no comfort for the girl save such as she could glean from the gentle attentions and kindly words of the Count.

At last she gave up all hope, and resigned herself to the bitter conviction of Hugh Gregory's guilt. Her mother's conviction was the same. So Hugh Gregory's name ceased to be mentioned in that house. Mary found, however, that crime could not kill love. She loved Hugh Gregory still—it was a love that would not down. But she could never marry him, she said. Let come what might, now, she said; she no longer cared what destiny might be in store for her.

As the weeks rolled on she learned to like the Count, for she came nearer to finding rest in his society than in any other.

It would take long to detail the beggings, beseechings and worryings which ended at last in wearing out Mary Gray's resistance and compelling her consent to marry Count Fontainebleau. Possession of the wealth which had come to Mary by the death of her uncle—and thus to all the family—only whetted her father's desire to climb higher and be allied to foreign nobility. The matter of appointing the wedding day was broached. Mary said, wearily:

"Name it yourselves. It is nothing to me. Only give me a little time to rest."

The 29th of June was appointed, the wedding to be strictly private, in John Gray's house. From that day forth, Mary Gray ceased to go outside the door or see anyone but the family and the Count. The news of the day, and the village gossip were never referred to in her presence. There was but one thing promised by the future which had interest for her. She had been assured that Hugh's trial would be delayed for a year or two by lawyers' shifts, and that he would probably not outlive that time, for his health was already failing, somewhat.

But in truth the trial came on very shortly. This fact was kept from Mary. The verdict of guilty was delivered on the 22d of June. The day appointed for the hanging was the 29th—the wedding day!

Confusion! What was to be done? Delay the wedding? No. It would not be necessary. The whole village was in a tumult of distress. David Gray had been generally detested, Hugh Gregory universally beloved. The people had brought themselves to expect only a verdict of manslaughter, and imprisonment. Already messengers were flying across country toward the capital; unquestionably there would be a long reprieve, possibly a free pardon. Then wherefore delay the marriage? Mary knew nothing of the verdict, or even of the trial.

CHAPTER SEVEN

IT WAS AN UNCOMFORTABLE GROUP THAT SAT TOGETHER IN John Gray's house late in the morning of the 29th of June, for all but Mary knew that no reprieve had come. It made even John Gray shudder to think of conferring an unsuspecting girl in marriage upon a man she did not love while the man she did love was walking to a shameful death. Mrs. Gray had been in bed ill, during a week, crushed with the dread of the possible miscarriage of the reprieve or pardon. The old clergyman had refused to officiate, and a passing stranger had been brought to serve in his place. He had been received at the door by John Gray and cautioned not to mar the joy of the occasion by any reference to the sad affair progressing in the village. The stranger said, in a guarded voice:

"You did not need to caution me. No one could speak of such a thing at such a time as this. I came by the gallows. All the people were collected there. None were unmoved; all the women and some of the men were crying. That young man was standing upon the gallows, between the sheriffs, the rope swaying in the wind over his head. He was pale and emaciated, but he stood erect like an honest man. And he spoke, too. He proclaimed his innocence. He said that his were the words of a dying man, and that in the sight of God he was guiltless. Voices all about cried out, 'We believe you, we believe you.' Twice he said he was ready, and the sheriffs took hold of the noose and the black cap, but both times a great shout arose of 'Wait, wait, for the love of God! the reprieve will come, the pardon will come!' Then everywhere I saw people mounted upon wagons and branches of trees, shading their eyes with their hands, and gazing away off over the prairie, and saying every little while, 'There! isn't that a man on horseback?—no—yes—away yonder is certainly a black speck—surely that is a horse!' But it was always a disappointment. At last the sheriffs drew the black cap down over the poor lad's face, and such a wail as went up from the people! I could not stand it. I fled. Ah how they loved that poor soul, how the mother-hearts there pitied him!"

The minister and John Gray entered the parlor. A blessing was invoked, then Mary stood up, pale and listless, between Count Fontainebleau and her father. The marriage service proceeded:

"None were unmoved; all the women and some of the men were crying."

"Hubert Count Fontainebleau, do you take this woman to be your lawfully wedded wife, promising to love honor and cherish her until death shall you part?"

The Count bowed his head.

"Mary Gray, do you take this man to be your lawfully wedded husband, promising to cleave unto him, to—"

For some seconds a far-off sound had been murmuring in the ears of the company, and rapidly growing in volume, as if its cause were approaching. It now burst into a succession of mighty cheers, close at hand, and in another moment a mob of shouting villagers came pouring into the house, with Hugh Gregory and the sheriffs in the van.

With a single glance Mary Gray read the whole blissful truth in Hugh's eyes, and the next instant she was in his arms. In the same moment the sheriffs seized Count Fontainebleau and manacled him. John Gray had to look his inquiries—he was dumb with stupefaction. A sheriff said:

"Never mind—it's all right. This devil done that murder. He had a pal, and the pal weakened and peached when he see Hugh just going to swing off. Told the whole story; and just as he was winding up, here comes a reprieve from the Governor. I'm intruding here, now, because of course the first man I wanted to see was this duck."

Hugh said:

"This devil done that murder!"

"There is no need of my explaining why this is the first place *I* wanted to come to and display the face of a guiltless man!"

The minister was modestly moving away.

"Stop!" said John Gray. "Let the marriage go on! Stand up, Mary Gray and Hugh Gregory, and may I die the death if I ever draw another mean breath while my name is John Gray! Here comes the old woman; everything's complete, now, minister—tie the knot and tie it tight!"

Chapter Eight

The Count's Confession

UNDER SENTENCE OF DEATH FOR THE MURDER OF David Gray, which I committed one year ago, I make this true record of my life. My name is Jean Mercier. Born in a village in the south of France. My father was a barber. I learned and followed the trade a while. But I had talent and ambition. Without help from anybody, I gave myself a sort of universal education. I learned many languages, made good success in the sciences, and became a good deal of an inventor and mechanic. I learned navigation at sea. By and by I tried my hand as a guide—a courier. I carried tourists all about the world. At last, in an evil hour, I fell into the hands of a Monsieur Jules Verne, an author. Then my troubles began. He paid me a great salary, and sent me here and there and to and fro in all sorts of disagreeable vehicles, and then he listened to my adventures and made each of my journeys into a book. That would have been all right if he had confined himself to the facts; but no, nothing would do him but he must spread. He turned my simple experiences into extravagant and distorted marvels. This humiliated me beyond expression, for I was very sensitive in the matter of truth and honest dealing—at that time. All my friends knew how I was employed; they believed that those atrocious stories had been set down just as I had spoken them—and one by one they ceased to recognize me—they regularly cut me. I remonstrated with M. Verne repeatedly—it did no good. This monster sent me down the Seine in a leaky old sand-barge; when I came back, he listened to my tale and went to work and spread it out into that distresséd book called "Twenty Thousand Leagues Under the Sea." Next he bought an old second-hand balloon and sent me up in it. The old bladder went up about two hundred yards and then collapsed, and I fell in a brick-yard and broke my leg. The literary result of that trip was the book called "Five Weeks in a Balloon"—the heartless fraud! He sent me one or two more little foolish flights in that ragged thing and wrote extravagant books about them. Well by and by he sent me from Paris all the way to a beggarly town at the very tail end of Spain, in an ox-cart. I was nearly a year on the road, and almost died of low spirits and starvation before I got back. What was the result? Why, "Around the World in Eighty-five Days!" He patched up his miserable balloon, and sent me one more

"I hove him out of the balloon!"

trip. I stuck fast in the clouds over Paris without budging, for three days, waiting for a wind, and then slumped down into the river, caught a fever and was abed upwards of three months. While I lay there I brooded over my miseries and by and by murderous thoughts became familiar to me—pleasant to me, I may say. When I got well he said he had fitted up the balloon in the most perfect way and was going to take the next voyage with me. I was glad. I hoped we might both break our necks. He put his valise, his fur coat and all his fine toggery into the balloon, along with a lot of provisions, liquors and scientific instruments. Just as we sailed he put into my hands his distortion of my last trip—a book entitled "The Mysterious Island!" I glanced into it—that was enough. Human nature could stand no more. I hove him out of the balloon! He must have fallen a hundred feet. I hope it killed him, but I don't know. Of course I didn't want to be hanged, so I hove out the scientific instruments to lighten ship; then I put on M. Verne's good clothes, and began to enjoy myself with his food and wines. But I had lightened ship too much. I went so high that sleep got the best of me, and presently insensibility. I never knew anything, after that until I woke up in John Gray's prairie in the midst of the snow. Do not know what became of the balloon. But I do know, by the dates, that I made the trip from France to Missouri in two days and twenty-one hours. And John Gray will understand, now, how I managed to travel across his prairie without leaving a track—he was always curious about that, poor man; but I judged that if I told him it would wander away and get into print, be wafted to France, and then some meddler would want to know if this ballooning foreigner might not be able to shed some light upon M. Verne's last moments.

I concluded it would be best for me to take a fictitious name and stick close to Deer Lick the rest of my days; but I could not abide the idea of teaching school forever for a living. So when I happened to hear that David Gray had put Mary Gray into his will for his entire property, I tickled her father with my false foreign wealth and grandeurs, and began my courting. One day David Gray left me alone in his office a moment, and I rummaged around, and found a will giving the whole property to a distant relative of David's instead of to Mary. My love cooled, and I went straightway and told Mary I would try to tear my love out of my heart, for her sake. But when Gregory and David Gray quarreled in my presence I discovered that I had been spying out an old will and that there was a newer one which would still leave the property to Mary. So I once more resolved to marry Mary, and I knew I could do it.

That unpleasant old Mr. Gray would be alive now, and I would be patiently waiting for him to drop off in a natural way, if he had not been so foolish as to swear he would go home and make a new will disinheriting Mary. It seemed to me best that he should take a berth with his fathers right away. Murder comes easy to a man whose mind has been unsettled by tortures such as M. Verne had inflicted upon me. I at once hired an accessory to keep watch at David Gray's door while I disposed of that person. I was to give this assistant a farm. He has only himself to thank that he is not a landed proprietor in this most charming and intellectual community of pious hog-raisers to-day. Well, at midnight I borrowed a knife of Mr. Gregory—that provincial sleeps like a gravestone and snores like a locomotive—and in fifteen minutes David Gray had retired from active pursuits. He had just begun his new will—and if, from that day to this, I have been thanked by Mr. and Mrs. Hugh Gregory for permanently interrupting that document in its very first sentence, the circumstance has escaped my memory. I got a bad scratch or two on my hands, in the struggle, but I always wore gloves, (a custom which I had all to myself in this artless region,) wherefore these were not seen by anyone. I returned Mr. Gregory's knife to him—at least I put it in his bed; then I borrowed a piece of his coat tail to put with the corpse, and after bidding him a good-night, which he answered with a snore, I put a few little blood stains on his pantaloons and took my leave. I knew there were no brains in the community, therefore the hidden knife and the blood stains would be damning evidences against that snorer. Brains would have said, 'None but a fool would leave blood on his clothes and hide his knife in his bed-tick, let alone call attention to the hiding place with a blood-spot.' Farewell, good hog-cultivators, I am willing to go, being filled with a consuming desire to ask the late Monsieur Verne how many chapters of his "Eighteen Months in the Furnace" he has written, and whom he employs to stump around and gather the facts while he toasts himself in his private apartments and exaggerates them. Moreover, I want to know where he lit when he fell.

—*Mark Twain*

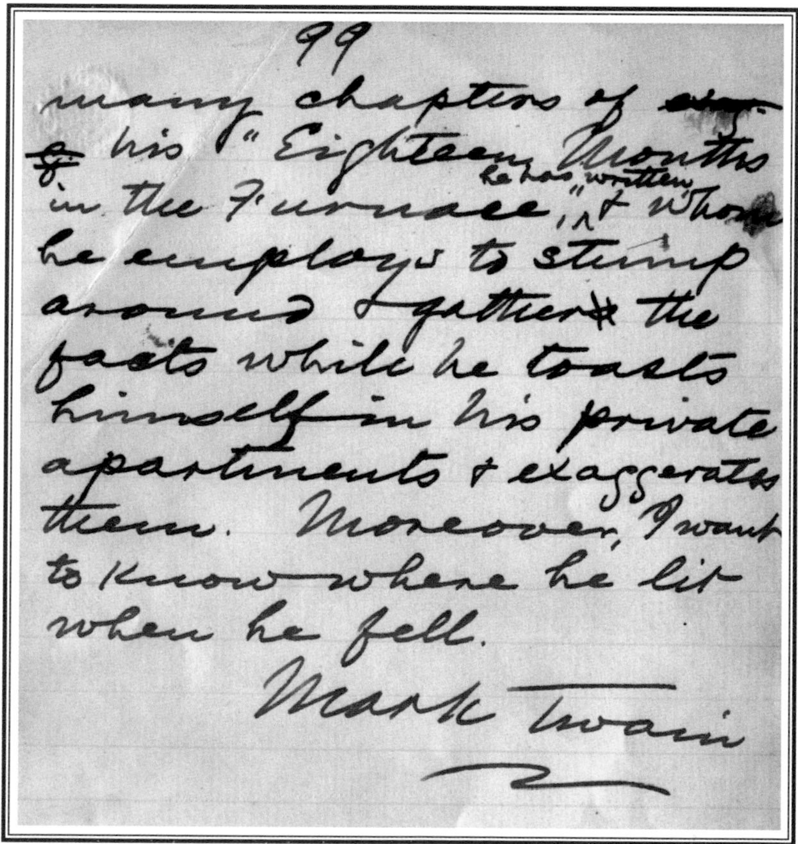

99

many chapters of ~~his~~
~~of~~ his "Eighteen Months
in the Furnace," he has written, & whom
he employs to stump
around & gather the
facts while he toasts
himself in his private
apartments & exaggerates
them. Moreover, I want
to know where he lit
when he fell.

Mark Twain

AFTERWORD

by Roy Blount Jr.

T*HERE'S* A NUB OR SNAPPER FOR YOU—DUMPING THE BURden of guilt into the lap of Jules Verne, and Verne overboard into thin air—leaving open the possibility of a sequel set in either Hell or France, which in Twain's Francophobe mind were similar. Postmodern, we might call this fusion of unrealistic fiction and unobjective criticism.

And yet, that snapper has been followed for 125 years by silence. If by any chance Twain has found himself, to his own surprise, in heaven, he may be looking down on us now, irritably, wondering whether he will *ever* be able to look up from that story with mock-innocent mock-surprise, triumphant in having sprung true surprise upon the truly unsuspecting.

As it is, the reader may just be left wondering what Twain had against Jules Verne. We will come to that. The reader may also be wondering why the whole story is marked by ill (in more than one sense) humor. It hardly seems to spring from the same imagination that had so recently been producing the friendship of Huck and Jim and the following portrait, in Huck's words, of the late teenage mortuary poet Emmeline Grangerford: "Every time a man died, or a woman died, or a child died, she would be on hand with her 'tribute' before he was cold. She called them tributes. The neighbors said it was the doctor first, then Emmeline, then the undertaker—the undertaker never got in ahead of Emmeline but once, and then she hung fire on a rhyme for the dead person's name, which was Whistler. She warn't ever the same, after that; she never complained, but she kind of pined away and did not live long."

What was bugging Mark Twain in 1876, to make him think up the benighted village of Deer Lick? He had already become perhaps the nation's most famous writer. He was ensconced—happily, for a time—in a mansion (resembling a steamboat) in Hartford, Connecticut, with his well-born wealthy wife and his first two daughters. Thanks to the influential Howells, Twain had also won critical recognition as far more than a wild western humorist.

In 1869 Howells, then an assistant editor, had taken the unusual step of reviewing in the *Atlantic*, with great enthusiasm, a book distributed not by a respectable publishing house but by the more commercial means of advance subscription peddled door-to-door.

Aside from a collection of sketches that had attracted little notice, it was Twain's first book, and one of his best: *The Innocents Abroad.* "I had the luck," Howells later recalled, "if not the sense, to recognize that it was such fun as we had not had before." Twain, clad in a sealskin coat with the fur side out, paid an unannounced visit to the staid Boston offices of the *Atlantic* to thank the anonymous reviewer, and a warm friendship commenced that would last until Twain's death in the next century.

Howells also drew Twain's work into the pages of the *Atlantic*, which Twain appreciated because, as he put it, "it don't require a 'humorist' to paint himself striped and stand on his head every fifteen minutes." Aside from publishing "A True Story" and other short pieces, Howells had encouraged Twain to write for the *Atlantic* a series of reminiscenses about his days as a riverboat captain, "Old Times on the Mississippi," which would later make up the best part of one of his best books, *Life on the Mississippi.* Early in 1876 Howells had vetted the manuscript of *Tom Sawyer*, which would be published (and praised by Howells in the *Atlantic*) later that year.

Howells and his young son John spent the weekend of March 11 at the Twain mansion in Hartford. Howells wrote to his father that when John "found the black serving-man getting ready for breakfast, he came and woke me. 'Better get up, Papa. The *slave* is setting the tables.' I suppose he thought Clemens could have that darkey's head off whenever he liked." It was probably during that weekend (a day or two after Alexander Graham Bell, incidentally, got the first telephone to work) that Twain proposed an editorial package. He and Howells would work up a "skeleton" plot and have twelve authors each "write a story, using the same plot, 'blindfolded' as to what the others had written." On the April 2, Howells wrote less expansively to the novelist Thomas Bailey Aldrich, another friend of Twain's, who would become Howells's successor as editor of the *Atlantic*: "I send also a scheme of Mark Twain's which we shall carry out if we can get any one to help. That is he and I will write a story on the proposed basis, if you and two or three others will do so."

On April 22, Twain wrote to Howells that he had gone ahead and written, in two days, a full-blown version of the story. On April 26 he wrote again to Howells, "Mrs. Clemens says my version of the blindfold novelette . . . is 'good.' Pretty strong language—for her. However, [her remark] is not original. God said the same of another Creation."

On April 28, Howells wrote back: "Aldrich was here today, and we talked over the Blindfold Novelette business. But we've neither of us begun ours. Can't you send me yours?"

Twain's May 1 response was both a bit pushy and defensive:

> *Here is the "Blindfold Novelettes." You will see that I have altered it as we contemplated. The most prominent features in the*

story being the Murder & the Marriage, the one name will aptly fit all the versions. Then the thing will read thus in the headings:

"A Murder & a Marriage. Story No. 1,"

You could add to this screed of mine an editorial bracket to this effect—

"Messrs. Howells, Trowbridge, etc., have agreed to furnish versions of this story, but it is also desirable that any who please shall furnish versions of it also, whether the writers be of literary fame or not. The MSS offered will be judged upon their merits & accepted or declined accordingly. The stories should be only 8 or 10 Atlantic pages long—Ed. Atlantic."

Something of that sort, you know, to keep people from imagining that because my name is attached to the proposition, the thing is merely intended for a joke.

Presumably what Twain sent then was the skeleton outline, for on May 4 he wrote again that he was coming to Boston and "I'll bring my Blindfold Novelette, but shan't exhibit it unless you exhibit it yours. You would simply go to work & write a novelette that would make mine sick. Because you would know all about where my weak points lay. No, Sir, I'm one of those wary old birds!"

What happened over the summer with regard to this project is not known. In June Sitting Bull's Sioux wiped out General George Custer's cavalry at Little Big Horn. On the Fourth of July America celebrated its centennial. Later that month, Hayes accepted the Republican nomination. In August, Twain set aside the novel he had been working on for the past month. "I have written 400 pages on it—therefore it is very nearly half done", he wrote to Howells. "It is Huck Finn's Autobiography. I like it only tolerably well, as far as I have got, & may possibly pigeonhole or burn the MS when it is done."

He had not cooled off, however, on the novelette scheme. On August 23 he wrote Howells, "We must get up a less elaborate & a much better skeleton-plan . . . & make a success of that idea. David Gray spent Sunday here & said we could but little comprehend what a rattling stir that thing would make in the country. He thought it would make a mighty strike."

Who was David Gray? "The gentlest spirit and the loveliest that ever went clothed in clay, since Sir Galahad laid him to rest," according to Twain. They had begun a lifelong friendship in 1870, when Twain was living in Buffalo, New York, where Gray was a subeditor at the *Buffalo Daily Courier* and Twain was a contributor to, and part owner of, the rival *Buffalo Express*. With $25,000 leant him by his future father-in-law, Jervis Langdon of Elmira, New York, Twain had bought into the *Express* in 1869, by way of settling down for marital life. When Sam Clemens married Olivia Langdon and moved into a Buffalo mansion bought for the couple by Jervis, Gray and his family became the Clemenses' only intimate friends in that city. The Buffalo roots did not hold—Jervis Langdon came down with stomach cancer and died, Olivia fell ill and nearly died, her houseguest Emma Nye stayed on to nurse her and came down with typhoid fever and died, and Olivia delivered a premature and never healthy child, Langdon Clemens, who would live for only nineteen months. Twain sold out his interest in the *Express* for only $10,000 and moved the family to Hartford. But they remained close friends with the Grays. Why, then, would Twain appropriate his name, in this "mighty strike" of a story, for an "irascible," "generally detested" murder victim?

Let us note that the narrator of Twain's *A Connecticut Yankee in King Arthur's Court* lassos Galahad off his horse. The real-life David Gray was pious and neurasthenic, but a good sport. He was also, like Orion Clemens, a Tilden supporter. In their correspondence Twain and Howells joke that this was a sure sign Tilden would lose. Gray's poetry was rather like the example of Emmeline Grangerford's given in *Huckleberry Finn.* He must have been the sort of innocent, like Orion only with money, whose chain Twain loved to pull on. Gray seems to have been the first person to whom he showed a sketch he had written, set in the court of Queen Elizabeth II, "which shook . . . Gray's system up pretty exhaustively." This sketch would be printed privately in 1880 as *1601. Conversation, As It Was by the Social Fireside, in the Time of the Tudors*, a bit of ribaldry which is pretty much one fart joke after another. Then too, gray is an uninspiring mixture of black and white.

In October Howells wrote that he wasn't having any success generating interest among other writers. He suggested that Twain simplify the plot. Twain said he would. "All it needs is that the hanging & the marriage shall not be appointed for the same day. I got over that difficulty, but it required too much MS to reconcile the thing—so the movement of the story was clogged." Later that month, Twain wrote again:

> *I see where the trouble lies. The various authors dislike trotting in procession behind me. I vaguely thought of that in the beginning, but did not give it its just importance. We must have a new deal. The Blindfold Novelettes must be suggested anonymously. Warner says, let this anonymous person say his uncle has died & left him all his property—this property consisting of nothing in the world but the skeleton of a novel; he does not like to waste it, yet cannot utilize it himself because he can't write novels—in which way he hopes to get 6 or 8 novels in place of one, & thus become wealthy.*
>
> *Now I would suggest that Aldrich devise the skeleton-plan, for it needs an ingenious head to contrive a plot which shall be prettily complicated & yet well fitted for lucid & interesting development in the brief compass of 10 Atlantic pages. My plot was awkward & overloaded with tough requirements.*

Warner will fill up the skeleton—for one. No doubt Harte will; will ask him. Won't Mr. Holmes? Won't Henry James? Won't Mr. Lowell, & some more of the big literary fish?

If we could ring in one or two towering names beside your own, we wouldn't have to beg the lesser fry very hard. Holmes, Howell, Harte, James, Aldrich, Warner, Trobridge [sic], Twain—now there's a good and godly gang—team, I mean—everything's a team, now.

Nearly three years later, in April of 1879, Twain was still writing to Howells, "Can't you get up a plot for a 'skeleton novelette' & find two or three fellows to join us in writing the stories? Five of us would do. I can't seem to give up that idea." Five years after *that*, he was pushing the idea, unsuccessfully, on the *Century* magazine and George Washington Cable. What was the fascination?

He had begun a similar sketch, and set it down in his notebook eleven years earlier, in July of 1868 (the same month that the Fourteenth Amendment to the Constitution granted citizenship to former slaves). The narrator is "John L. Morgan, of Illinois, a farmer & a man of good reputation." He tells of finding, on a plain covered by fifteen inches of snow, an emaciated man who does not look like an American. Morgan figures "He was too weak to hold his horse, & has been thrown from a wagon or from the saddle." And yet "there was no sign of wheel, hoof or boot anywhere around."

The stranger is carried to the farmer's house. A doctor is summoned and neighbors gather, advancing theories as to how such a thing can have happened—"The spiritualists came to the conclusion that the spirits brought the man there, & this seeming to be the most reasonable idea yet advanced, spiritualism rose perceptibly in the favor of unbelievers." The stranger awakes and begins to speak in an unknown tongue. The schoolmaster arrives, diagnoses it as French, and translates. The stranger is Jean Pierre Marteau, who ran away from his village home at sixteen and went to sea. Unjustly, he was convicted of a killing. After nearly seven years as a galley slave and several failed escape attempts, he was on a work detail in Paris when, under guard, he came upon a crowd around "an immense balloon swaying about, . . . made fast to the ground by a rope. A man was making a little speech. He begged the multitude to be patient . . . The balloon was distended with gas, & struggling to get away. An idea flashed liked lightning through my brain. I tore loose from the guard, snatched the hatchet from his hand, threw my tools into the car, jumped in & cut the anchoring rope with a single stroke!

"Whiz! I was a thousand feet in the air in an instant."

There the notebook entry ends. Later Twain added a note: "While this was being written, Jules Verne's 'Five Weeks in a Balloon' came out, & consequently this sketch wasn't finished."

Verne's international bestsellerdom began with *Five Weeks in a Balloon.* Can Twain's obsession with the skeleton-plot project have derived from resentment over Verne's inventing science fiction just as Twain was getting his balloon off the ground? In 1878 Twain tried to discourage Orion from writing an imitation of Verne: "I think the world has suffered so much from that French idiot that they could enjoy seeing him burlesqued—but I doubt if they want to see him imitated." Some fifteen years later, Twain himself tried to burlesque *Five Weeks in a Balloon*. In *Tom Sawyer Abroad*, he sent Tom, Huck, and Jim up in a balloon with a character called The Professor, who falls overboard over the Atlantic. It is a bad book. At any rate Twain was a highly competitive author, much given to putting himself up against others.

Which brings us to that "good and godly gang." In *The Adventures of Tom Sawyer*, the book that Twain had most recently finished, Tom makes a great production of organizing himself, Huck, and their friend Joe Harper into a band of pirates. They steal away from their homes, commandeer a raft, and float down the Mississippi to an island. Joe and Huck keep getting tired of the game, but Tom rallies them, especially after he slips back home, eavesdrops, and is gratified to learn that everyone in the village thinks the boys have drowned. Instead of showing himself and dispelling his poor Aunt Polly's grief, he goes back to the island and keeps the gang together for a couple of days until they can show up triumphantly at their own funeral, just as the entire congregation has been reduced to tears. Tom thereby wins affection from Aunt Polly, the envy of other boys in school, and the heart of Becky Thatcher. At the end of the book, Tom is planning a new gang, of robbers. "A robber is more high-toned than what a pirate is. . . . In most countries, they're awful high up in the nobility—dukes and such." Huck has escaped from the civilizing clutches of the Widow Douglas, but he agrees to give respectability another try when Tom tells him it is the only way he can be included in the new gang.

Huck is Twain's disreputable and good-hearted side; Tom, his manipulative, reputation-hungry side. James Russell Lowell and Oliver Wendell Holmes were the crème of eastern literary society, Aldrich a rising figure in those circles, Howells the nation's leading literary arbiter. Bret Harte had been Twain's mentor when the latter was learning to write out in California, and had preceded Twain to literary recognition and fame in the East. John T. Trowbridge was best known as the author of "Darius Green and His Flying Machine," a whimsical poem about a farmboy trying to impress his peers by constructing, and taking off from a barnyard loft in, his own set of wings. (That poem's last lines, "On spreading your wings for a loftier flight, / The moral is—Take care how you light," rather resemble the last words of *A Murder, a Mystery, and a Marriage*.) But Trowbridge was also a longtime contributor to the *Atlantic* and the author of serious books, including one that recounted his tour of the South right after the war—he saw farmers literally plowing around corpses. Charles Dudley Warner was coeditor of the *Hartford Courant* and an established author with whom Twain had recently collaborated in writing *The Gilded Age,* a satire on Reconstruction-era corruption. If Twain had managed to get all these big and middling fish "trotting in procession behind me," he would have set himself at the head of just about every considerable literary element in America at the time. Oh, and Henry James was the only young writer who attracted from Howells anything like the fond support he conferred upon Twain. (In 1888 Howells and Twain would coedit *Mark Twain's Library of Humor*, an anthology including selections from every one of these writers, except the most profoundly humorous of them all, James: nineteen selections from all of them together, six from Howells, twenty from Twain himself.)

Can any sane person, we may ask, have expected to get Henry James's juices flowing with a plot abounding in bumpkins, spleen, assault, and battery? In a story by Henry James, it would not be a European fallen into America but an American popping up in Europe; and, if, yet, in some sense, falling, then not onto a prairie of all things but—if alfresco, indeed, must be—into, or rather in, the charming garden of a richly paneled estate of a woman dressed all in black—but a black that strikes the observer's needle eye as light and transparent—a woman, in fine, who knows something that may well be evil, for all that she does not "turn" a "hair"; and *if*, after all, indeed fallen, *not* fallen, in any case, from a balloon. People do not fall from, having never had a priori the faintest of inclinations to clamber into, balloons in stories by Henry James. Nor are they stabbed, by knives (glances, yes); if they die at all they expire of causes no more heavily definite than, *comme on dit*, something socio-somatic, assuming that in any very much more coarsely corporeal sense than the psychological they for that matter have in the first place "lived," at all, if to live is to be negotiably up to whatever it is that Europeans . . .

Consider, in Twain's story, this sentence:

"It was a man."

That, in a story by Henry James, would not, as the master himself might put it, "do." Nothing so rude, nothing so uninflected, nothing so blockily unductile—nothing, in short, so short—would serve.

But here we are thinking in terms of the mature James. As of 1876 James was still early. His style had not yet attained the subtlety of even *The Bostonians*, about which Twain wrote Howells in 1885 that he "would rather be damned to John Bunyan's heaven" than read it—much less into the daunting complexity of the later fiction, in which even Howells rather lost interest (as he never did in Twain's). James had published readily readable ghost stories in the *Atlantic*. What made Henry so fine that he wouldn't want in on a project of Mark's?

Twain/Clemens had a lifelong fascination with pairs (often a good boy set off against a bad boy), twins (Siamese, preferably), dream selves, doubleness, imposters, opposites joined. He and James (the latter was eight years younger, lived six years longer) were the great heads and tails of American fiction in the late nineteenth century. And neither wanted to be tails. Twain's personality, prose, and humor were outgoing, broad, and visceral; James's introverted and refined. Twain creates a great illusion of speech happening before us on the page; James, of cogitation. Twain loved to draw powerful people into his orbit, as James was eminently sensitive enough to realize. The two met several times over the years. After their first encounter, in London over dinner in 1879, James wrote to Howells that Twain was "a most pleasant fellow, what they call here very 'quaint.' Quaint he is!" This was the year after James published *Daisy Miller*, portraying a surpassingly charming and above all innocent American girl whose ingenuousness brings her to grief abroad. In 1900 James reported in a letter to his sister Alice that in a recent conversation Twain had offered "a muddled and confused glimpse of Lord Kelvin, Albumen, Sweden and half a dozen other things," but the confusion—though Twain's drawl no doubt had a good deal to do with it—was mostly James's: Twain had been referring not to Lord Kelvin but to a fashionable Swedish osteopath named Kellgren.

"A little touch" of this confusion, writes Leon Edel, "would be imported into *The Ambassadors* in the character of the dyspeptic Waymarsh. This hypothesis gains some credence when we discover, in James's original plan for the novel, that the character was first named Way*mark*. The 'sacred rage' of Waymark-Waymarsh has in it perhaps a touch of the sacred rage of Mark Twain." Lambert Strether, the central character of James's 1903 novel *The Ambassadors*, is much like James himself: detached from life but tremulously sensitive to the faintest social vibration, like the boy in school who never quite gets the whole guy thing and therefore notices everything. Sam Clemens was a sickly, bookish child and a nervous, delicately built man. Howells took note of his "taper fingers and pink nails, like a girl's, and sensitively quivering in moments of emotion." Twain's lifelong bent for mischief and adventure may have been a semi-conscious effort not to be such a fellow as Strether.

The rich American woman Strether hopes dispassionately to marry sends him to Paris to see about her son, Chad Newsome, who she fears is associating with a Frenchwoman of the world. Waymarsh, a fellow American abroad, is a gruff, unsubtle ("The only tone he aimed at with confidence was a full tone") former congressman (irony there, Twain having defined Congress as America's only native criminal class) who indeed resembles Twain physically—"the great political brow, the thick loose hair, the dark fuliginous eyes." At one point Strether sees Waymarsh "looking out, in marked detachment, at the Rue de Rivoli . . .—it was immense how Waymarsh could mark things."

"Oh, he's much more in the real tradition than I," says Strether, and "He's a success of a kind I haven't approached." (Twain's books made lots of money, James's precious little.) Waymarsh "doesn't understand—not one little scrap," says a worldly Miss Barrace. "He's delightful. He's wonderful."

Very belatedly, Strether figures out ("Is she bad?") that Chad is indeed caught up, chipperly, in chic adultery. And although Strether is shocked as well as fascinated, he doesn't interfere, though this means sacrificing his own marital future. Realizing that he himself has missed out on life, he proclaims to youth—in the person of Chad's friend, an icky self-described "little artist-man" named Little Bilham—that a person should go ahead and "Live!" (*The Ambassadors*, according to James, was inspired by a similar bit of advice conferred on a real young man by the comparably timid Howells.) Waymarsh, whom Strether has never quite trusted, blows the whistle on him to Chad's mother, and winds up as the conquest—in some nebulous Jamesian sense—of the distinctly unappealing Mrs. Pocock, from back home. So it wasn't Twain who managed to co-opt James, but *au contraire.*

Twain, writes Edel, was "the historian and embodiment of a kind of American innocence" that James "devoted his lifetime to studying." In *A Murder, a Mystery, and a Marriage*, the words "innocence," "guiltless," "guiltlessness," "pure," "purity," "simple-hearted," "unsuspecting" and "artless" appear, altogether, fifteen times; "guilt" or "guilty," three. A fallen man in the midst of pure driven snow tries to impose guilt on an honest man, but innocence wins out. Not only was Twain's first big book *Innocents Abroad*, but the book of his own that he pronounced his favorite, *Personal Recollections of Joan of Arc*, celebrated at great stultifying length the innocence of the maid of Orléans. And he dubbed his house in Redding, Connecticut, the one he died in, "Innocence at Home," until his daughter made him change it to "Stormfield."

Several elements in *A Murder, a Mystery, and a Marriage* will recur in the last half of *Huckleberry Finn.* The intrafamily feud evokes the interfamily one between the Grangerfords and the Shepherdsons. Twain set the novel aside just before that feud flared into violence. The fake Count presages the greatly more memorable King and Duke. Hugh Gregory's belated violent response to continued insults anticipates Sherburn's shooting of Boggs. The fallen balloonist is, in effect, a runaway slave. And in both works innocence condemned is vindicated in the nick of time. One moment in the story resonates, inconspicuous as it is, throughout Twain's writing. It is when the preacher brings glad tidings, he thinks, and John Gray responds with an embarrassing silence, and Mrs. Gray begins to come out with "*Our* great news—," and her husband shouts, "Hold your tongue, woman!"

And "the simple mother shrank away, dumb . . . , and then the clergyman made his way out of the place with as little ease and as little grace as another man might who had got a kick where he looked for a compliment."

"If I could only *know* when I have committed a crime," Twain once wrote to Howells. "Then I could conceal it and not go stupidly dribbling it out, circumstance by circumstance, into the ears of a person who will give no sign till the confession is complete; and then the sudden damnation drops on a body like the released pile-driver, and he finds himself in the earth down to his chin. When he supposed he was merely being entertaining."

Innocence slapped down. In *Huckleberry Finn*, Huck finds Jim weeping with remorse. He is remembering the time when he told his little daughter to shut the door.

> *"She never done it; jis' stood dah, kiner smilin' up at me. It make me mad; en I says agin, mighty loud, I says:*
>
> *" 'Doan' you hear me?—shet de do'!'*
>
> *"She jis' stood de same way, kiner smilin' up. I was a-bilin'! I says:*
>
> *" 'I lay I* make *you mine!'*
>
> *"En wid dat I fetch' her a slap side de head dat sont her a-sprawlin'. Den I went into de yuther room, en 'uz gone 'bout ten minutes; en when I come back, dah was dat do' a-stannin' open* yit, *en dat chile stannin' mos' right in it, a-lookin' down and mournin', en de tears runnin' down. My, but I* wuz *mad, I was agwyne for de chile, but jis' den—"*

The wind slams the door shut, and the child doesn't blink, and Jim realizes that scarlet fever has left her "deef en dumb—en I'd been a-treat'n her so!"

Twain's work is full of such moments. Huck's father beating him for no reason. (Huck's response is rather affectless, like Orion's letter about being abandoned by his audience.) Aunt Polly slapping Tom Sawyer when it was his pious brother Sid who broke the sugar bowl. (Tom, characteristically, finds this excuse for self-pity "morosely gratifying," even in the long run empowering—he establishes his "nobility" later by taking a licking in school for something Becky Thatcher did.) A late, maudlin story, "A Dog's Tale," is narrated by a dog who drags the family baby away from a fire in the nursery but is beaten by the father (another Mr. Gray), who, not having noticed the fire yet, thinks the dog is hurting the baby. "I did not know what I had done," sighs the dog, "yet I judged it was something a dog could not understand, but which was clear to a man and dreadful."

Twain's way of telling a story risks deadly silence for the satisfaction of slaying the audience. A benign exploitation, a roughhouse disabuse, of innocence: the misdirection, the pause as the audience wonders "what th' . . . ? and then, bang, the snapper. The rug pulled out from under the unsuspecting—in such a way as to *lift*, after a moment of suspension in thin air, the victim's spirits. In writing, that sort of rhythm can be sustained, and renewed, over the course of a sentence, paragraph, sketch, or episode, but it isn't plot. Plot requires a larger structure and a somewhat quieter and more resounding resolution. What is wrong with Twain's "skeleton novelette" project is that plot, the macromechanics of a work, is what he was worst at. *A Murder, a Mystery, and a Marriage* is the only thing he ever wrote, I believe, whose events are resolved in the venerable comic-plot tradition: by marriage. Indeed, the title suggests a traditional three-part structure, and the story seems to bear the title out, only the mystery—where this stranger came from—comes first. And doesn't really have much bearing on the murder and the marriage. Then, after the marriage, the restless narrative comes back to the original mystery by taking off after Jules Verne.

Twain's books tend to digress in all directions, except when held together for a while by some unimposed force like the Mississippi River. His stories are sketches or anecdotes, his novels episodic and unshapely. In life he was fascinated by machines, but they did not agree with him—he went bankrupt backing a marvelous typesetting machine that fizzled. He was at his best—America's unequaled comic master—when language carried him along. "As long as a book would write itself," he once reflected, explaining why he set *Huckleberry Finn* aside, "I was a faithful and interested amanuensis and my industry did not flag, but the minute that the book tried to shift to *my* head the labor of contriving its situations, inventing its adventures and conducting its conversations, I put it away and dropped it out of my mind."

Perhaps he didn't want anything, even a book, to be what he was afraid *everything*—the death of his younger brother, the death of his sickly son, the death of his favorite daughter—was: his fault. In his dark moods, he would blame God for not existing. (His extremely distant father died when he was eleven.) In general, he expected women, and Howells, and America, to coddle him. (His mother was fun-loving and relatively indulgent, his wife called him "Youth.") The humorous storyteller's strategy, as Twain writes, is to feign innocence so as to trip up the audience's. Perhaps the deeper purpose is to preserve the humorist's own. Was his story project a joke he hoped, consciously or unconsciously, to pull not so much on Jules Verne as on his American literary rivals? Was that why he was so determined to slip them a skeleton? Then stand back, innocently, and watch them wrestle with it? Were they wary of being sandbagged by his balloon?

Or was he struggling with some skeleton of his own? The tone of this story is anything but ingratiating. In the interrupted notebook sketch, the townspeople who wonder at the man in the snow are unsophisticated but amiable, and open to outside information. They are not to be dismissed as people whose "hearts," to quote Twain's summary of Deer Lick's citizens, "were in hogs and corn."

Laurence McCain, one of the few critics who has given much attention to *A Murder, a Mystery, and a Marriage*, argues that it is the turning point in Twain's attitude toward the village of his boyhood.

McCain points out that before this story, notably in *Tom Sawyer*, the fictional small towns Twain modeled after Hannibal, Missouri, are "drowsy and peaceful," a challenge for a mischievous boy but infused with "communal virtue and harmony" in the light of which the boy hero wins universal approval. In *The Gilded Age* (1873), the inhabitants of Hawkeye, Missouri, are, in Twain's words, "uncouth and not cultivated, and not particularly industrious; but they were honest and straightforward, and their virtuous ways commanded respect." In *Old Times on the Mississippi* (1875), he describes Hannibal as a "white town drowsing in the sunshine of a summer's morning," enlivened suddenly by the gladsome arrival of a steamboat. In the first half of *Huckleberry Finn*, as Henry Nash Smith notes, "The image of Hannibal has lost its magical power to generate the sense of security that defines Tom [Sawyer]'s world. The dream of innocence has not entirely vanished, but is now associated not with the town but with the natural setting."

Whereas everything in Deer Lick, except the snow and the featureless young lovers and the nick-of-time reprieve, is squalid. And the villagers Huck Finn encounters the rest of the way down the river are mean, cowardly, greedy, lazy . . . .

What happened?

Let's look at the evolution of Twain's politics. When the Civil War broke out, shutting down commercial steamboat traffic on the Mississippi and ending his career as a pilot (since he did not want to be impressed into military transport duty and be shot at from both sides of the river), he joined a volunteer brigade of the Confederate Army. After two weeks, he lit out for the far western territories, where he stayed until the fighting was well over. His politics right after the war may be inferred from entries in his notebook for 1868, just before and after the interrupted fallen-balloonist sketch. Before it, among notes from his recent voyage to California, we find his freewheeling interpretation of an uprising in the Colombian province of Panama (which he had crossed by train). American business interests, afraid that the Colombian government was about to seize the railroad,

> *hurried down to Panama with a cargo of wines & liquors, & at the end of 3 days had everybody drunk, a riot under way, the seeds of a promising revolution planted, & the Pres in prison. Result, the renewal of the lease to the Amer Co for 99 years, for $1,000,000. There is nothing like knowing your men.*
>
> *. . . all it is necessary to do is to cry Viva Revolucion! at head of street, & instantly is commotion. Doors slammed to, 50 soldiers march forth & cripple half dozen niggers in their shirt tails, a new Presi. is elevated, & then for 6 mos (till next Rev) the proud and*

happy survivors inquire eagerly of new comers what was said about it in Amer & Europe.

After the sketch, and a joke involving Indians and mustard, comes this with regard to domestic politics:

> *Political parties who accuse the one in power of gobbling the spoils, &c, are like the wolf who looked in at the door & saw the shepherds eating mutton & said—*
>
> *"Oh certainly—it's all right as long as it's* you*—but there'd be hell to pay if I was to do that!"*

At that time the national political parties were the economy-minded Democrats and the more ideological Republicans. The Democrats were dominated by Southerners, big-city political machines, the Irish and other Northerners who had been unenthusiastic about the war effort (the Irish, because they couldn't afford to avoid the draft) and had no desire to press Reconstruction. The radical Republicans controlled Congress, which had impeached and nearly deposed Lincoln's successor, Andrew Johnson of Tennessee, because he didn't want to punish the South or grant full citizenship to former slaves. The Republicans elected Ulysses S. Grant, former commander of the Union Army, to succeed Johnson in 1868. Twain the wild westerner had no dog in that fight.

But then he settled in Buffalo to marry a woman from a staunch abolitionist family. For Livy he swore off liquor and tobacco (temporarily). He would "quit wearing socks," he said, "if she thought them immoral." Her father set him up financially. The literati around the *Atlantic* were solidly radical Republican. And so became Twain. Grant, whom he may have met briefly in late 1867, became his hero. And in fact he did take an interest in the Hayes-Tilden race, the first presidential campaign, he said, that he had cared about one way or the other. In August of 1876, Howells wrote him that he was working on a campaign biography of Hayes, who was his wife's first cousin. Twain wrote back that Hayes's letter to the Republican convention accepting its nomination "was amply sufficient to corral my vote without any further knowledge of the man." He had been asked by Democrats in Jersey City "to be present at the raising of a Tilden . . . flag there & take the stand and give them some 'counsel.' Well, I . . . gave them counsel & advice . . . as to the raising of the flag—advised them 'not to raise it.' "

"Why don't you come out with a letter, or speech, or something, for Hayes?" replied Howells. "I honestly believe that there isn't another man in the country who could help him so much as you."

Twain wrote back that he might, but not "until the opportunity comes in a natural, justifiable & unlugged way; & shall not then do anything unless I've got it all digested & worded just right. . . . When a humorist ventures upon the grave concerns of life he must do his job better than another man or he works harm to his cause." But—losing all hesitancy—he urged Howells not to forget the skeleton-plot project. A few days later Twain wrote Howells to joke that Hayes ought to appoint an old poet friend of Twain's—"poor, sweet, pure-hearted, good-intentioned, impotent" Charles Warren Stoddard—to a consulship because he has "no worldly sense," and advised Howells that Hayes's victory was assured because the mercurial Orion had suddenly become a Democrat, and possibly a "Mohammedan."

On September 30, Twain did make a brief speech at a Republican rally in Hartford. According to newspaper accounts, he said he represented "the literary tribe" who usually stayed out of politics but were backing Hayes because he stood for good government and a civil service system based on merit, not political connections. "Our present civil system, born of General Jackson and the democratic party, is so idiotic, so contemptible, so grotesque, that it would make the very savages of Dahomey jeer and the very god of solemnity laugh. . . . We even require a plumber to know something [laughter, and a pause by the speaker] about his business [more laughter], that he shall at least know which side of a pipe is the inside." Yet "we put the vast business of a custom house in the hands of a flathead who does not know a bill of lading from a transit of Venus [laughter and a pause]—never having heard of either of them before," and entrusted the Treasury Department to "an ignorant villager who never before could wrestle with a two-weeks' wash-bill without getting thrown." The diplomatic corps, he said, spoke only English and that by way of "flourishing the scalps of mutilated parts of speech." There was even an ambassador "whose moral ceiling has a perceptible shady tint to it."

Howells wrote him that he had made a big hit. Republican and Democratic newspapers alike had quoted his speech. And "Lowell was delighted with your hit at plumbers."

"Of course the printers *would*," Twain responded, "leave off the word 'gas-' from 'pipe' in my remark about the plumbers, thus marring the music & clearness of the sentence."

On election day, Twain wrote Howells that the inconclusive returns coming in made him "lift up my voice and swear." Bret Harte, who had been his houseguest off and on for months (they had been writing a play together, and wearing out their friendship), astonished Twain by appearing to be "the only serene and tranquil voter in the United States." Harte's explanation was appalling: through connections, he had been promised a consulship by both Hayes and Tilden. He couldn't afford to vote at all, he said, because he might by chance vote for the loser and the winner might find out. That was his only interest in the matter. Twain remained "an ardent Hayes fan." Howells wrote to his father back in Ohio that Twain was "the most [confirmed] Republican I have met in a long while; hereabouts, you know, they are a very lukewarm brotherhood."

Indeed they were, with regard to Reconstruction (if not plumbers). By 1876 the Republican Party had already lost interest in imposing that skeleton plot on the South. Hayes's nomination-acceptance letter, which had so impressed Twain, made that clear even as the election began. Hayes campaigned for reconciliation, which meant the North and the South getting together again on grounds of white supremacy.

In *The Gilded Age*, Twain and Warner had portrayed the Colonel Sellers character as delighted by the opportunities Reconstruction opened up—for graft. He wants to sell Tennessee land to the government to build a college for freed slaves, because, as Ward Just has written about the novel's portrait of the period, "'There's public money available for any project with 'Negro' or 'Indian' attached to it. The mantra throughout the book is the cry, 'There's millions in it!' " Twain might blame corruption in government on Jacksonian Democrats, but the public quite reasonably associated it with the scandal-ridden Republican administration under Grant. In 1873, the sort of corruption and greed satirized in *The Gilded Age* had contributed to a financial panic and a severe national depression. Accordingly, voters in the 1874 congressional elections had replaced a 198–88 majority in the House of Representatives with a

169–109 Democratic one. In 1876 the Republicans were running scared. And as David W. Blight puts it in his recent book *Race and Reunion*, "No true national consensus ever gathered around the cause of black liberty and equality except as it was necessary to restoring and reimagining the Republic itself. But Americans generally had run low on imagination about racial matters by [1876]."

What the Republicans wanted was to reconstruct their party. What white America wanted was to reconstruct the Union. And what Mark Twain wanted was to reconstruct himself.

As soon as Hayes was declared the winner, Twain was trying to lobby the White House, through Howells, for political appointments to people he knew (upstanding ones, to be sure). None of his candidates got anything. And when Twain heard that Harte, whom he had come to despise, was indeed under consideration, he denounced him in a letter he had Howells forward to Hayes. Howells, taking care that Twain should not hear about it, in fact put in a good word for Harte, who got a consular position in Germany. Twain was beside himself. "Harte," he wrote to Howells, "is a liar, a thief, a swindler, a snob, a sot, a sponge, a coward, a Jeremy Diddler, he is brim full of treachery, & he conceals his Jewish birth as carefully as if he considered it a disgrace. . . . To send this nasty creature to puke upon the American name in a foreign land is too much." He felt "personally snubbed" that the president had "silently ignored my testimony."

In fact, Harte's character (and writing) had deteriorated considerably, and would continue to, but he needed a job. Twain's needs were greater—he needed for America to hang on his word, which meant working out some sort of politics higher-minded than resentment of Bret Harte but less quixotic than demanding to know whatever happened to the goals of Reconstruction.

In office, Hayes bore out Henry Adams's assessment of him as a "third-rate nonentity." When the Republicans nominated James Garfield in 1880, Twain made a speech for him, and followed it with another one that made fun of both sides. Then after the election Twain wrote to remind Garfield that he'd backed him and to urge that the great runaway slave and abolitionist orator Frederick Douglass, whom he described as "a personal friend of mine," be kept on as marshal of the District of Columbia. Douglass wrote Twain to thank him. In a speech to the Republican convention of 1876, Douglass had asked, "Do you mean to make good to us the promises in your constitution?" By 1880 he knew the answer: no. He described himself as a "field hand" for the Republican Party. Twain, for his part, had positioned himself well.

Then Garfield was assassinated and replaced by his vice president, Chester A. Arthur—whose involvement in civil service corruption Twain had mocked, implicitly, in his 1876 speech for Hayes. Who needed that sort of affiliation? In 1884 Twain found a stance from which he could make fun in all directions: he became a lifelong mugwump. The Republican candidate for president, James Blaine, had been implicated in shady financial dealings. His Democratic opponent, Grover Cleveland, had fathered a child by a woman to whom he wasn't married, which disqualified him in Howells's eyes, but Twain wrote Howells, "To see grown men, apparently in their right mind, seriously arguing against a bachelor's fitness for President because he has had private intercourse with a consenting widow! Those grown men know what the bachelor's other alternative was [prostitutes, presumably]—& tacitly they seem to prefer that to the widow. *Is*n't human nature the most consummate sham & lie that was ever invented?"

Be that as it might (generally, in public, Twain was bluenosed about sex), he forsook his party to vote for Cleveland, whom he chose to see as the candidate of reform. In so doing, Twain joined a good and godly gang indeed. They included President Eliot of Harvard and Charles Francis Adams, of the Boston Adamses. Derided in the popular press as "little Mugwumps," *mugquomp* being an Algonquin Indian word for "chief," they began to call themselves mugwumps with pride. The label suited Twain right down to the ground. It had a funny sound to it, and it connoted innocence. "We, the mugwumps, a little company made up of the unenslaved of both parties," he recalled in his *Autobiography*, "had no axes to grind."

Cleveland won, and Twain paid him a visit. Cleveland told him a joke. In *A Connecticut Yankee in King Arthur's Court,* the narrator, Hank Morgan, hears the same joke from a knight. "It was one which I had heard attributed to every humorous person who had ever stood on American soil, from Columbus down to Artemus Ward. It was about a humorous lecturer who flooded an ignorant audience with the killingest jokes for an hour and never got a laugh; and then when he was leaving, some gray simpleton wrung him gratefully by the hand and said it had been the funniest thing they had ever heard and 'it was all they could do to keep from laughin' right out in meetin'.' That anecdote never saw the day that it was worth the telling, and yet I had sat under the telling of it hundreds and thousands and millions and billions of times, and cried and cursed all the way through." Morgan has the knight hanged.

Twain had a friend in the diplomatic corps whom he wanted to recommend to Cleveland—but how could he do so and "save my mugwump purity undefiled"? His soluton was to address a letter in his friend's behalf to Cleveland's daughter Ruth, not yet two years old. Cleveland assured him in a personal letter that the friend would keep his post.

When Twain's own favorite daughter, Susy (on whom he modeled his portrait of Joan of Arc), was writing, in her teens, a biography of her father, she asked him for a statement about himself and he said, "I am a mugwump and a mugwump is pure from the marrow out." In a speech in 1900, he would refer to himself in the third person as the last mugwump left, "a GRAND OLD PARTY all by himself." By that time the Republican president was a whipper-snapper named Teddy Roosevelt, whose imperialism Twain scorned. (He called TR a Tom Sawyer type.) Democratic-leaning publications that had tended not to give him much attention were now asking for interviews, which he granted liberally, on issues of the day. Sometimes, in interviews and in writing, he vented outrage against oppression of the weak, but generally the oppressors he attacked were in other countries. He wrote a blistering book-length attack on "The United States of Lyncherdom," but agreed with his publisher that he'd better not put it out in his lifetime, for fear of alienating Southern book buyers. (It came out in 1923.)

By 1906, when he was dictating the long autobiographical ramblings that have still not been published in full, his aspersions were on mankind in general—though he argued that human nature couldn't help it, that mankind was a machine shaped by forces it couldn't control. His thinking on the 1876 election had swung around to the point that he looked back on its outcome as "one of the Republican party's most cold-blooded swindles of the American people, the stealing of the presidential chair from Mr. Tilden, who had been elected, and the conferring of it upon Mr. Hayes, who had been defeated. . . . . I have since convinced myself that the political opinions of a nation are of next to no value, in any case."

Reconstruction didn't figure into his recollection. After he died in 1910, muttering something about Jekyll and Hyde, the nation mourned. The last words of Howells's tribute, *My Mark Twain*, set him not among but above every writer Twain could have wanted to gang up with: "Emerson, Longfellow, Lowell, Holmes—I knew them all," wrote Howells, "and all the rest of our sages, poets, seers, critics, humorists; they were like one another and like other literary men; but Clemens was sole, incomparable, the Lincoln of our literature."

But by failing to respond as we might expect to the historical moment of 1876, hadn't our literary Lincoln failed to carry on the truth of the Emancipation Proclamation? No. In 1876, as a national consensus sloshed a reconciliationist glaze over the issues left unresolved in the aftermath of slavery, Mark Twain's writing began—in *A Murder, a Mystery, and a Marriage*—to grow darker. He began to acknowledge that the roots of his innocence were in a village corrupted by slavery. In the second half of *Huckleberry Finn*, good-natured people are abused over and over by meanness, callousness, and violence. Throughout the rest of his writing career, America's greatest humorist's great pursuit was to snatch empathetic comedy from the jaws of intentional and unintentional cruelty. Many of his contemporaries achieved great popularity by writing nostalgically about a culture of slavery. We can see right through their work today. And by today's standards Twain's racial attitudes are often embarrassingly still under construction—but his writing hangs on to a raw innocence that burns away smugness. The radical Republican Reconstruction was an imposed plot that wouldn't take hold. Mark Twain's personal reconstruction is tricky, awkward, and still alive.

In *Huckleberry Finn*, just before Twain took his hiatus, Huck plays a mean trick on Jim. Huck has been separated from the raft in a storm, and Jim has gone to sleep grief-stricken because he thinks Huck has drowned. When Jim wakes up and finds to his delight that Huck is back on the raft, Huck convinces him that he dreamed the whole storm and everything. When Jim realizes that his good nature has been taken advantage of, he tells Huck "*trash* . . . is what people is dat puts dirt on de head er dey fren's en makes 'em ashamed."

"It was fifteen minutes before I could work myself up to go and humble myself to a nigger—but I done it," Huck says, "and I warn't ever sorry for it afterwards."

Jim's joy, Huck's cruelty, Jim's credulousness, Jim's indignation, Huck's pride, and Huck's apology and relief—all different forms of innocence bouncing off of one another on a field of shame.

Twain's obsession with innocence was no mere literary convention. It was cheekier, funkier, wetter, more nearly heart-to-heart—potentially more *embarrassing* in a fresh sort of way—than the

"Transcendental" idealism that had flourished in Concord, Massachusetts, before the Civil War. The difference between, say, Thoreau's wit and Twain's humor is the difference between a cat's pounce and a young dog's jump-up. The difference between Thoreau's darkness and Twain's (though Twain *admired* cats, and at some level was as crafty as Thoreau) is the difference between a cat's reserve and a dog's remorse.

Thoreau was against slavery, and knew nothing of African-American culture. Twain was imbued with both. The conflicts within Twain's sensibility no doubt arose from childhood issues, but for him slavery was such an issue. One night when he was four, he was kept awake by the groans of a runaway slave who'd been captured, beaten, and tied up in a shack near his house. While still a boy he was out in a boat on the river when the mutilated body of another slave rose to the surface before his eyes. In 1896 he was checking into a Bombay hotel when "a burly German" who worked there saw a hotel servant doing something to his dissatisfaction and

> *without explaining what was wrong, gave the native a brisk cuff on the jaw and* then *told him where the defect was.... The native took it with meeknesss..., not showing in his face or manner any resentment. I had not seen the like of this for fifty years. It carried me back to my boyhood, and flashed upon me the forgotten fact that this was*

> *the* usual *way of explaining one's desires to a slave. I was able to remember that the method seemed right and natural to me in those days . . . ; but I was also able to remember that those unresented cuffings made me sorry for the victim and ashamed for the punisher. . . . When I was ten years old I saw a man fling a lump of iron-ore at a slave-man in anger, for merely doing something awkwardly. . . . It bounded from the man's skull, and the man fell and never spoke again. He was dead in an hour. I knew the man had a right to kill his slave if he wanted to, and yet it seemed . . . somehow wrong. . . . Nobody in the village approved of that murder, but of course no one said much about it. . . .*
>
> *For just one second, all that goes to make the* me *in me was in a Missourian village, on the other side of the globe . . . and the next second I was back in Bombay, and that native's smitten cheek was not done tingling yet!*

Murder, mystery, and—between North and South, black and white, First World and the Third—a marriage of sorts. After the Civil War Twain moved through his connection with the *Atlantic* to purge himself of the stigma of Southernness—*not his fault*—that tainted him in the eyes of respectable literary society. Then he found that America, from Boston on out, wanted to forget the shame of slavery. Deftly though he maneuvered to fix himself thereafter in the national mind, in *his* mind the shame rose more and more to the surface. "The skin of every human being," he wrote, "contains a slave." He could at least make America flinch before it laughed. He kept trying to reconstruct and deconstruct the smiting of innocence, and the shuddering silence that follows it.

About the Author

Born Samuel Langhorne Clemens on November 30, 1835, in the "almost invisible" village of Florida, Missouri, he was the sixth child of John Marshall and Jane Lampton Clemens—proud Virginia and Kentucky stock who no longer owned but only rented slaves. When Sam was nearly four the family moved to another Missouri village, Hannibal, on the western bank of the Mississippi, where he attended "the ordinary western common school" from age five until age twelve. His father died in the spring of 1847, when Sam was eleven.

Within a year his mother took him out of school and apprenticed him to a Hannibal printer, Henry La Cossitt. He became a printer, and when he outgrew his interest in setting type, he became a steamboat pilot on the Mississippi, his favorite profession long after the Civil War forced him to abandon it. When it did, he went west with his older brother and became, in time, a newspaper reporter in Virginia City and San Francisco, signing himself "Mark Twain," the leadsman's call for two fathoms. By 1867, when he was thirty-one, Mark Twain had published his first book, *The Celebrated Jumping Frog of Calaveras County, and Other Sketches*. In 1869 he proposed marriage to Olivia Louise Langdon and, with her father Jervis's financial help, bought an interest in the Buffalo *Express*. In 1870 they were married and moved into a fully furnished house in Buffalo, also provided by Jervis. Their first child, Langdon Clemens, was born there in early November 1870 but did not survive his second year. Jervis himself died in August 1870, and within a year of that event the Clemenses decided to move to Hartford, Connecticut.

In April 1876, at the age of forty, Mark Twain found himself married with two young daughters and half a dozen servants, living in Hartford, Connecticut, and making a handsome income from his books. His sketches and essays were also much in demand by the editor of the *Atlantic Monthly*, William Dean Howells. He wrote *A Murder, a Mystery, and a Marriage* on April 21 and 22 of that year, expecting Howells to publish it along with three or four stories by other well-known writers, who were supposed to make use of the same plot outline. That scheme never prospered and the story remained unpublished, but Mark Twain typically did not discard it. *The Adventures of Tom Sawyer*, his first novel about his boyhood in Hannibal, was to be published later that year, and he was just weeks away from beginning another story, also based in Missouri. Referring to this burgeoning work, he told Howells he liked the result "only tolerably well, as far as I have got, & may possibly pigeonhole or burn the MS when it is done." Eight years later he completed the manuscript and decided to call it *Adventures of Huckleberry Finn*.

In the eight years it took him to complete that masterpiece, Clemens and his wife had a third daughter, Jean. In the meantime, Mark Twain wrote and published three other large books: *The Prince and the Pauper* (1881), *A Tramp Abroad* (1880), and *Life on the Mississippi* (1883). He began to invest time and money in an automatic typesetter invented by James W. Paige and then founded his own publishing house, Charles L. Webster & Company, through which he published *Huckleberry Finn* and his next book, *A Connecticut Yankee in King Arthur's Court* (1889), as well as books by other authors—most notably, the two-volume *Memoirs* of one of his heroes, Ulysses S. Grant. But the Paige typesetter was never quite the success Clemens was sure it would be, and when the Panic of 1893 forced his publishing house into bankruptcy, he had to abandon his dream of fabulous wealth and treat the debts of the firm as his own.

He published *The Tragedy of Pudd'nhead Wilson* (1894) and *Personal Recollections of Joan of Arc* (1896) before undertaking a speaking tour around the world to earn money to pay off those debts, reporting on that trip in his last large book, *Following the Equator* (1897). The Clemenses' eldest daughter, Susy, had stayed at home while they traveled. At age twenty-four, Susy died of meningitis while her family was still in England. They never again lived in Hartford, returning instead to New York City in October 1900. Mark Twain's wife, Olivia, died in Florence in 1904. His youngest daughter, Jean, died from an epileptic seizure on Christmas Eve, 1909, and Clemens himself died from heart failure in Redding, Connecticut, on April 21, 1910.

Five years before publishing *Huckleberry Finn*, Clemens was asked if he would be willing to "be a boy again and start fresh." His answer was *no*, except under certain conditions. "The main condition would be that I should emerge from boyhood as a 'cub pilot' on a Mississippi boat, & that I should by & by become a pilot, & remain one." He had several further "conditions," but the most interesting was a frank requirement that he also "be notorious among speakers of the English tongue" and be known to all as "the celebrated 'Master Pilot of the Mississippi.' " On being recognized in that way, he supposed, "I should feel a pleasurable emotion trickling down my spine & know I had not lived in vain." In spite of Clemens's hindsight, to someone like Rudyard Kipling there was no doubt what sort of "master" Mark Twain really was. In 1903 Kipling said, in a letter to Frank Doubleday, "I love to think of the great and God-like Clemens. He is the biggest man you have on your side of the water by a damn sight, and don't you forget it."

—*Robert H. Hirst,*
General Editor, Mark Twain Project

CONTRIBUTORS

ROY BLOUNT JR. grew up in Decatur, Georgia, and attended Vanderbilt University and Harvard before working as a reporter and columnist for the *Atlanta Journal* and moving to New York to write for *Sports Illustrated.* Throughout his career, he has contributed to 122 publications, including the *Atlantic Monthly, The New Yorker,* the *New York Times, Esquire, Gourmet,* and the *Oxford American.* His work has been anthologized in such collections as *The Best of Modern Humor, The Elvis Reader, The Ultimate Baseball Book,* and *The Sophisticated Cat.* His sixteen books include *Crackers* (1980), *First Hubby* (1991), *Be Sweet* (1998), and, with photographer Valerie Shaff, *If Only You Knew How Much I Smell You* (1998). He is the editor of *Roy Blount's Book of Southern Humor* (1994), which brings together 152 selections from the writings of Mark Twain, Louis Armstrong, Flannery O'Connor, Charles Portis, and many other Southerners. Blount also appeared Off-Broadway in a one-man show, *Roy Blount's Happy Hour and a Half,* and is a regular panelist on National Public Radio's *Wait, Wait . . . Don't Tell Me!* His biography of Robert E. Lee will appear in 2002. Blount currently resides in Mill River, Massachusetts, and New York City.

PETER DE SÈVE was born in New York in 1958. He began drawing as a child, inspired by the comic books he collected, as well as by science fiction and fantasy illustration. At Parsons School of Design he was introduced to contemporary and nineteenth-century American and European illustration, all of which continue to inform his style. In his twenty-year career, de Sève has been published by nearly every major magazine in America, including *Time*, *Newsweek*, *Atlantic Monthly*, *Smithsonian*, *Forbes*, *Premiere*, and *Entertainment Weekly*. He also contributes covers frequently to *The New Yorker*. In recent years, de Sève has designed posters for Broadway plays, as well as characters for numerous animated feature films produced by Disney, Dreamworks, Pixar, and Blue Sky Productions. Credits include *The Hunchback of Notre Dame*, *The Prince of Egypt*, *Mulan*, *A Bug's Life*, *Tarzan*, and the upcoming *Ice Age*. His work has been exhibited widely in the United States and Europe, through such venues as the James Cummins Gallery (New York, one-man show, 1995); the Norman Rockwell Museum (Stockbridge, MA, group show, 1996); the Museum of American Illustration (New York, one-man show, 1997; annual group shows); and Teatro (European traveling group show, 1999–2001). He lives in Brooklyn, New York, with his wife, Randall, and daughter, Paulina.